This is a work of fiction. Names, characters, places, and incidents either are the product of the author's imagination or are used fictitiously. Any resemblance to actual events, locales, organizations, or persons, living or dead, is entirely coincidental and beyond the intent of either the author or the publisher.

Calling His Bluff: a Club Raven novel
By BA Tortuga
Copyright © 2017

Evil Plot Bunny LLC
PO Box 722
Loughman, FL 33858

Cover illustration by Erin Dameron-Hill
Published with permission

ISBN: 978-1-942831-39-6

First edition.
Printed in the USA

Calling His Bluff
A Club Raven Novel
by BA Tortuga

Calling His Bluff: A Club Raven Novel

Calling His Bluff

Chapter One   7
Chapter Two   11
Chapter Three   18
Chapter Four   20
Chapter Five   27
Chapter Six   30
Chapter Seven   37
Chapter Eight   46
Chapter Nine   54
Chapter Ten   58
Chapter Eleven   72
Chapter Twelve   88
Chapter Thirteen   90
Chapter Fourteen   99
Chapter Fifteen   103
Chapter Sixteen   123
Chapter Seventeen   130
Chapter Eighteen   154
Chapter Nineteen   160
Chapter Twenty   171
Chapter Twenty One   183
Chapter Twenty Two   202

Calling His Bluff: a Club Raven Novel
By BA Tortuga

Chapter One

The crack in the looking glass grew with every tick of the clock that heralded his doom. This morning it had bloomed in the bottom left corner, at first the tiniest chip, almost a hiccup next to the frame.

Now, five hours later, it climbed the glass, shattering Patrick's image into a mish-mash of scars and torn dress uniform.

He dropped his throbbing head into his hands, wishing for the thousandth time today that it had been him lost on the battlefield, that he had been the one carried off, bent and snapped in two, not his twin brother. Not the golden one. Not Henry.

His parents' cruel disappointment was like a draught of bitter almond. Then there was the situation in which he found himself today. Marrying. A woman. His brother's precious fiancée, in fact.

Carolina MacDonald was a lovely girl from a fine family, a pretty little debutante with a charming smile and a gentle manner. A good catch. A superb specimen of womanhood.

Too bad he didn't care a whit for the fairer sex. The thought of bedding her and producing offspring made his balls shrivel. Worse than that, his nights were filled with horrors, with screaming demons that battered at his very soul. He stood, his blouse soaked through with sweat, shudders rocking him.

He swallowed convulsively, the nausea worse than it had ever been on the battlefield, even when his sergeant had lost an arm to a ball when standing right next to him.

A single knock came to the door of his dressing room, preceding his father's scowling face, as unwelcome as it was unwelcoming. "The carriage leaves for the church soon and your lady mother wishes to see you. Good God, boy. Have you bathed yourself wearing your suit?"

"It's hot, Father." He knew it was unbecoming, but the cold sweat and the shakes refused to stop. "I am decent, if she wants to join me."

He felt the drag of his father's attention, the weight of disappointment and disapproval immense. "Pull yourself together. You act as if you're being sent back to the battlefield."

"Better that than this fresh hell."

"Stop being so dramatic. Marriage is nothing if not necessary. Get yourself together."

"I have no wish to marry Henry's betrothed, Father!" How difficult was this to comprehend? He did not desire to follow in his father's footsteps, acting the Lord of the Manor over the poor souls that slaved in the mill, the farmers who brought their cotton.

"Well, you're the only son I have left and you will damned well do as you're told." His father's ears went red, a sure sign of impending doom.

He had been the one who'd spent his childhood on horseback, riding through the fields and exploring, not learning the family business, nor scheming for position and place of power.

Now he was trapped.

The mirror crackled as if it was straining at the confines of its frame.

"You are no longer a child. Since you didn't have the common decency to die in your brother's stead, you will become what he had intended to be."

He clenched his hands into fists to keep from hitting his father in the face. When he looked, really looked, his father had become old, the lines in his face deep, the gray in his hair like tufts of cotton.

"I will work at the mill, I will do your will there, but to stand in front of God and make a promise to Henry's affianced?"

"By God, you will do this for your mother or I will disown you and have you tarred and feathered like a runaway slave!"

"I don't suppose I have to remind you that your side of the argument lost?" Not that they had fought a single soldier—Union or otherwise. He and Henry had been on the western front, fighting the damned heathens that threatened to take their land, their children.

"Never remind me that you would have given away our entire way of life." His father reached out, fingers like an iron band around Patrick's arm. "Now do your goddamned duty."

The muscles ground against the bone and something deep, deep inside him snapped, the mirror shattering and glass spraying through the air.

His father cursed, staggering away from him, hands over his face. "You little fuck! What did you do?" His father's voice rose to a shattering shriek, the fear plain.

His eyes were wide and he saw the world spin as if it moved outside him. Like a tornado had touched down right outside, the windows bowed in, then out, the heavy glass panes creaking and popping. A wild sound began to whisper inside him, echoing in the pit of his stomach and clawing its way up his backbone to settle in the base of his skull.

Patrick screamed, fingernails digging into the back of his head, tearing at his hair, at his scalp.

The windows exploded.

The door flew off its hinges.

His father rose up off the floor before slamming back against the wall.

"Isaac! Patrick! Jesus, help us!" His mother's voice came from a vast distance, a deep, dark hole.

He couldn't reach her, couldn't do anything. The storm held him immobile; all he could do was stand there and let it rage about him.

Black Jim, the man who had worked as head of the Daniels' house for as long as he remembered, appeared beside him like an ebony statue. "Patrick-boy. Sleep."

The blow to the side of his head was sudden, like a candle being snuffed out.

The silence that surrounded him was dark and utterly welcome.

Chapter Two

Lord love a duck, Canaan had a crick in his neck. The train ride from Texas had been… long. Real long. Still, he was glad he'd had a compartment and not some sitting up all the damned time seat. Especial with the Daniels' boy along for the ride.

The carriage was closed, too, keeping prying eyes out, so the transfer had been slick as snot. Now, he was sitting with his charge in the back lounge of Club Raven, waiting for the Colonel.

Laudanum had become Patrick Daniels' bosom chum, and Canaan had made it a point of pride to help continue the relationship. Now, it was going to be someone else's job to disassociate the man from it.

After all, coins crossed his palm to deliver goods. That was it. The parcel was safe and he had earned a fortnight of pleasure and relaxation, a mulled wine and an eye to watching the leaves turn in a cooler clime than the hell that was Texas.

The door opened finally, the Colonel striding in, his shadow close behind him. Seeing that damned Comanche always gave Canaan a chill.

Those black eyes saw things an indecent man might choose to keep hidden.

He stood, nodding. "Colonel."

They shook hands, Colonel smiling a bit. It didn't reach those bright blue eyes, but it made him a bit less intimidating. Then Colonel turned to study the unconscious man laid out on the long chesterfield.

"What's his tale?"

"Lieutenant Patrick Daniels. Father's a mill owner in Texas. Cotton. It was his wedding day and, apparently, he damn near razed an entire three-story house. Demons, they said, possessing him." Demons. Those idiots wouldn't know true demon-kin if they walked up and bit them on the ass, but that wasn't his place to say.

"Huh. Why is he here? If he's possessed his family needs to man up and kill him." The Colonel could be cold. Calculating.

"Matthias." It never ceased to amaze him, the wealth of emotion the Comanche could put into a single word.

"Because the man has not so much as a whiff of demon-kin in him, Colonel." The lad had been wide open, spread in front of him. He'd seen all Daniels' secrets. Hysteria? Absolutely. Loss of control? Completely. Utter guilt about his need for other men and the need to be controlled, to be on his knees? Perfectly. Possession?

Not even remotely.

"Well, damn. Would have made it easier. What do you reckon, then? What happened?"

"Lost a brother on the western front. Took a bullet himself to the back of the head dragging the other out and he doesn't remember a second of it. Lead poisoning? Haints?"

"I've seen stranger things." Colonel pursed his lips, then glanced at the heathen, whose name was Koni. "What do you think?"

"I think he is a danger to himself, my light."

"We need to put him in a secure place, then, until we think of what to do with him."

"Are you going to throw him in a hole?" That could be entertaining, genuinely.

"Careful, Canaan. Your truths are showing."

He grinned at Koni, winked playfully even as he fought a soft growl. "Nonsense. You don't get to play with my...truths."

"I do not want to."

"Not sure anyone does, old friend," Colonel murmured. "Help me move him and I'll find a servant to attend to him for now."

"Sure. So far he hasn't been the least bit aggressive. More addled, hmm?" Canaan headed over. Careful not to touch, he nudged the sofa. "Daniels. Daniels, you ready to go to your room, friend?"

Dazed pale blue eyes stared up at him, utterly lost. "We home again?"

"In a manner of speaking, yes."

"Oh." Patrick tried to rise, and Canaan stepped back to give him room. Touching might set the man off.

The big blond nearly tumbled over and Canaan caught him, stumbling under Patrick's weight.

Koni faded into the shadows, but Matthias stepped up, helping steady them both. "I got you, lad."

"Thank you, sir. I seem to have lost my feet."

"Not a problem at all." Colonel waltzed the man down the length of the room, heading to the back where they could access some private rooms.

"You got you a nice place here. I…"

Oh, don't let the lad think. That just made things worse.

"Thanks, son. Now, here's a place for you to lie down and rest some. Can I get someone to give you some water?"

Yes. Laudanum water.

The room they led Patrick toward was a maw, just an empty black space, and Canaan held back, his upper lip pulling back instinctually. He didn't like the dead feel of it, the way the noise in his head just stopped.

Colonel glanced back at him. "Send Lyle with water."

"No problem, Colonel. I'm on it." Anything to get away from that room.

Koni's laugh chased him as he made his retreat.

He found Lyle, who was one of Colonel's trusted servants. "Colonel needs laudanum and water in the dead room."

"Yessir. I've had your regular room made up for you, sir." The man was a walking mass of scars, one sleeve of his shirt as empty as one eye socket.

"You are a gentleman and a scholar." He started toward the stairs, but veered toward the billiard area instead. He wanted a brandy.

His job here was, in effect, done. Now he wanted to sit around and watch the crazed result of what he'd delivered.

He saw a few familiar faces in the billiard area, and one particularly friendly face at a card table. Remy Blanchard.

Oh, lovely. He did love that wicked gambler's smile. When Remy glanced up it appeared, one finger crooking at him.

That promised delicious fun and a healthy measure of wickedness. He approved. Canaan slid into the chair beside Remy. "Dealing solitaire?"

"No one wants to play with me, *cher*."

"That's a stone-cold shame. I will play." In fact, he thought he had quite the chit to play with.

"Well, now." Remy had golden eyes, like fine whiskey. Pretty man, with curly black hair and even white teeth.

"Indeed. You want to play for coin or favor?"

"Mmm." Remy looked him over. "Favor. I have plenty of money."

"And I can grant all sorts of favors."

"You certainly can." Remy shuffled the cards. "Tell me why you're here."

"I was making a delivery. Interesting, this one. Not demon, but dangerous."

"Indeed?" Those golden eyes lit up. Remy did love his danger.

"Indeed. Destroyed most of a house, three barns and half

of a cotton gin, not to mention terrifying some poor padre in a church."

"*Merde*." Black eyebrows winged up. "Now, that's something interesting."

"He's a pretty little package, too — all innocent lad in a grown man's body. But the need… His soul burns, aches to be played with."

"Are you trying to sell him to me, *cher*?" Remy dealt out a hand of cards. Five cards meant poker, or as Remy would call it, *poque*.

"You inquired. I responded." Remy was amazing, but not a love match. Simply a joyous interruption.

"Well, I shall have to make further inquiries once he's here a bit."

"Assuming the Colonel doesn't have him tarred and feathered." Like Remy would be able to wait. The energies were already drawing around Remy. Canaan could see them, spinning and whispering about his friend.

"Ah, Matthias. His bark is worse than his bite as long as no demons are involved."

"He does have particular prejudices, doesn't he?"

"Yes, indeed. Shall we play? I will ante up one favor."

"Mmm. One favor it is." He picked up his cards, pursing his lips while he perused them.

Remy watched him, the still, waiting posture he got while playing evident.

He had two pair, so he felt confident enough to smile. "Three chits to call in."

"My my. Listen to you. I will see your three and raise you one."

"Confident. Four it is. I need one card."

He exchanged his card, watching Remy take two. He got his full house, and he let his smile out.

"You look pleased," Remy said, cocking one brow.

"Do I?" He had to laugh, because that expression was so utterly Remy.

"You do. Your bid."

"Let's make it a half dozen."

"Hmm." Remy made a show of studying his cards. "I'll call."

"Fair enough. I have a full house, jacks high."

"Three of a kind. You pulled that, didn't you?" Remy chuckled warmly. "Well done."

"I did. How lovely is that. Again?"

"Certainly. Would you like to deal?" Remy pushed the cards to him.

"Oh, your trust stuns me."

"It should! I let few people touch my cards." The pause between the words *touch* and *my cards* made him smile.

He chuckled softly. "Sweet, barely-touched...cards."

Remy cackled like a giant bayou bird. "Pure as snow."

"I remember the first time you saw snow, Remy." It had been entertaining, to say the least. The silly man had slipped while running down the stairs and damned near busted his head.

"They have very little where you come from, as well, *cher.*"

He chuckled softly, leaned close and dared to nuzzle Remy's temple. "You do have a point."

"Let's find someplace else to play favors, shall we? A private room." Remy gathered the cards, tucked them away, then rose.

"You read my mind, dearest one."

"Oh, that would be a dangerous skill indeed."

Canaan chuckled. "It would. I imagine we have more than one member who can do just that." Club Raven boasted unique members.

"And I imagine they avoid your delicious brain like the plague."

He took Remy's hand. "I reckon so. I have too much in there."

They headed to the back, toward the huge African who stood at the doorway to the upper floors. Kwanele nodded, his expression never changing while he stepped aside to let them in.

"Thank you, sir." He nodded to Kwanele, who bared his sharpened teeth in a grin that was as horrifying as it was charming.

Remy chuckled. "I do love that man. Come along, *cher*. I'm working up a powerful hunger."

He did love the idea of Remy turning that hunger on him for a moment, letting him feel the weight of Remy's passion. Poor Remy felt everything, and the weight of others' happiness and sorrow must drag him down.

Fortunately for Remy, he was infinitely capable of taking anything the man had to give.

They reached a private room, the upstairs attendant unlocking it for them when Remy chose. Ah, Remy wasn't in the mood for games or toys. Just fucking.

"Come inside, dearest. I'll take care of you."

"Will you, *cher*? I'm needing in a powerful way."

He closed the door behind them, drawing Remy into a kiss that echoed the darkness that bubbled inside him. "You have my word."

Chapter Three

Patrick woke slowly, his head heavy, his chest feeling as if someone had piled bricks on him. He blinked, listening to his eyelashes click against his cheeks.

The darkness was broken by a single flame—a candle, not even an oil lamp—and even its flickering glow hurt his head.

He closed his eyes again, but he heard the slightest scrape of leather over stone and looked again. A man with a turban on his head and a poncho of some soft, white material came to stand in the tiny circle of light. "Water, sir?"

"Pl-please. Please." Was he in the hospital?

"Certainly." The man had a lyrical accent, sweet and high. The water was almost shockingly cold and he heard it splash as it hit his stomach, the liquid near refused, and he fought to keep it down.

"There now. I know it's difficult." Cool hands helped to ease him up to sitting, piling pillows behind him. "I have some crackers here if you're very empty."

"Yes. I'm sorry. Sorry, I don't...Where am I?"

"You are here." The man smiled, teeth very white against his darker skin. "I am Anek. If I may offer you anything, please call to me."

"Anek…" He blinked slowly. "May I have another drink?"

"Of course, Mr. Patrick. You have been sleeping very long."

"My family?" He had a vague memory of fire and glass, of a train.

"Your father was rather unwell for some time, but I

understand he is on the mend. You have letters from a young lady, but no other word."

A dull panic began to build within him, and he frowned, his heartbeat speeding.

"There is no need to read them now, is there?" Anek touched his shoulder, and he calmed immediately, his eyelids growing heavy.

"No. No, no need at all."

"I didn't think so." Anek patted his chest, and he yawned. "Sleep again, Mr. Patrick. I will bring soup to you in a bit."

"Yes, sir. Thank you."

"Sleep." Anek began to sing, a strange, almost Injun sounding song, but it soothed him, sending him toward his dreams.

His quiet, peaceful dreams. Wherever he was, please God, let him stay and sit a spell.

Chapter Four

S o, is he a demon?" Remy asked, peering at Anek from under his lashes. The East Indian stood in the kitchen, stirring tea leaves in boiling water with a strange whisk.

"Not even remotely, sir."

"No? Then why is he locked away, *ami*?" Remy liked Anek, and loved the sweet sugar and milk tea he created.

"He has a deep rage that bubbles inside him and no way to control it, Sahib."

"Hmm. What happens if he doesn't control it?" Ever since Canaan had arrived with the man in the dead room, Remy had been itching. Curious.

"Master Canaan said that he razed a house without raising a hand. He needs a firm base, yes. He has no family left that wants to keep him."

He knew Canaan had said that. He wasn't sure he believed it. How much rage would that require? "Can I meet him?"

Anek nodded, no hesitation at all. "He must remain in the room he is in."

"Of course." He would never go against one of the club owners when it came to safety. They knew what was best for the members, all of them. "I can take him some tea for you, *ami*."

"That would be a kindness. He suffers from the shaking sickness."

Laudanum wanted to become an eternal friend.

Remy nodded easily, which he hoped hid his eagerness. He had no idea why he was so keen to see this man, but he didn't question his impulses. They served him well and Canaan had whispered in his ear, soft and wicked, making luscious promises about the treasures he had seen in the lad's mind.

"He will not eat, but I will send food in case."

"Sure." He could sit with the guy. He'd take his cards. Tempt the lad into a game.

"Thank you." Anek flashed him a warm smile, and he grinned back. Anek's dark, liquid eyes reminded him of the Creole ladies back home somehow. Anek handed him a beautifully arranged tray, complete with a floating lotus blossom in a bowl. Wonderful frippery.

He nodded and left the kitchens, trudging along. Anek must have a spell or something to keep the tea warm, as far as it was from the kitchen to anywhere.

No fewer than six phantasms stopped him on the way, asking if he needed assistance.

Remy simply smiled and shook his head. He had a feeling about this one.

He wanted to keep this one for himself.

When he reached the room, he set the tray on the tiny table outside the door so he could use the key Anek had left by the tea. He tucked it into his waistcoat after he heard the lock click.

A broad shouldered man rested on a bed, bare to the waist, tan and warm against the white sheets. Remy paused, staring for a moment. Gracious. This one didn't look ill at all.

In fact, he looked like a Greek god, with golden hair curling about his ears, the barest halo of stubble framing his jaw.

He carried the tray inside, then returned to lock the door. There were protocols. Julian would be cross if he let the dangerous one escape. No one liked it when Julian was cross. One of the owners of Club Raven, Julian was from England, and he could be rather cutting.

The lad sat up, bright blue eyes popping open. "Hello? Mister Azle?"

"Anek, *bébé*, and no, I'm Remy."

"Oh." The man's cheeks went pink in the low, guttering lights from the candle. "Sorry, sir."

"Anek sent me with tea and soup."

"Thank you kindly." The voice was pure Texas, the drawl slow and sweet. Remy liked it. It wasn't home, exactly, but utterly familiar.

"Here. Have you had Anek's tea?"

"Yes, sir. It's plumb soothing."

He laughed softly. "It's something, all right. May I sit?" He indicated the edge of the bed, because Anek had put a mat of some sort on the floor, but there was no chair or bench.

"Yes, sir. Please. I should…I been sleeping a little bit, I think."

"Here, let me help you sit up." He lifted under— "What's your name?"

"Daniels. Patrick Daniels."

Oh, a Paddy. How charming.

"*Enchanté.*" Remy tugged under Patrick's arms and helped him sit up. "There we are. Do you need the chamber pot? There's one under the bed."

"Thank you. I can't— Do you know where my kit is? I seem to be lacking clothes. All of them."

"I'll have Anek bring you a nightshirt for now." Remy rather liked the lad naked. He liked naked men in general.

"I'd be mighty grateful."

He went to ring for Anek while Patrick did his business, giving the lad his privacy. He had to slip outside to do it, and the weight of the room Patrick was in slipped off him. Poor lad must be truly scary.

Anek appeared like smoke. "Yes, Sahib?"

"The lad needs something to wear — a nightshirt, maybe?"

"Of course. I will have a chair brought for you, as well. A small table."

"Mind reader." He said it in an admiring way, and Anek's mysterious smile made Remy laugh.

He went back in, the heavy blackness of the room's energy making him shiver. Patrick sat on the edge of the bed, sipping the tea, eyes watching him closely.

"Where is this place?"

"You're in Baltimore City. Do you know it?"

"Baltimore... I'm from Texas."

"Mmm. I am from the Crescent City, originally. I came here from San Francisco. We're all wanderers here."

The knock at the door made him spin back and answer. A chair, a table, a lamp and a nightshirt, excellent. "*Merci.*" Now he could sit and chat with the lad.

Patrick tugged the nightshirt over his head, managing well until he got caught up in the sleeves.

Remy leaned over to help, coming eye to eye with Patrick when the neck hole popped into place. "Better?"

"Thank you. I've wasted some."

"Have you?" *Merde.* What must Patrick look like at full health?

"I'm afeared so." Patrick sat heavily, a sheen popping out on the lad's forehead. "Thank you for the care."

"You need to eat. That will help get your strength back." Remy was hardly gifted with prescience but, for what he had in mind, Patrick would need all his strength. Every bit.

"This is the first morning I have felt the urge, I admit."

"There, you see?" He uncovered the rich broth Anek had sent. "Go slowly."

"Yes." The hand that held the spoon trembled, but managed the trip. "Mmm. This is good."

"You sound so surprised." Remy chuckled, delighted. "We have only the best here at Club Raven."

"Club...This isn't a sanatorium?"

"No, *bébé.* It's a good place, *vraiment?*" He reached out to help steady Patrick's hand, fingers on the bare skin of his wrist.

A buzz passed between them, and Remy had to wonder what lightning might have happened elsewhere in the club.

"Oh!" Patrick nearly dropped the spoon. "Don't let me spill on your clean shirt."

"The staff here is particularly good at removing stains." Preternaturally good, in fact.

"Do you live here, then?"

"No. This is a gentleman's club. You can stay here for a time, if you have difficulties, but most of us reside elsewhere." His own house awaited him on the harbor, for a fact.

"A gentleman's club... I-Somehow I seem to be confused."

"Do you remember the accident at all?" He watched Patrick carefully for any signs of agitation.

"The accident?" Patrick shook his head, fingers lifting to the back of his skull.

"Yes, *bébé*. You had one. Your people sent you here to recover. We have more resources." So willing to forget, this one.

"I was fixin' to have to get married. To my brother's woman." He could see a dull flush heat Patrick's cheeks.

"Now why would you do that?" That sounded like hell on earth. Remy assumed the brother had passed on, because Patrick was honorable. Law abiding. Remy felt those whispers deep down.

"He'd had her. Not in a bad way, but there wasn't no choice. I said she could just pretend to be Henry's widow, but..." There was a tremor that barely moved the bed.

"That sounds very sensible." He took the spoon, feeding Patrick more soup. "I'm an accomplished forger. I'll make her a certificate."

"I don't intend to marry."

"No, *cher*, that's what I mean. To say she was married to your *frère*."

"Yes. Because I won't do it. I ain't going back." The soup began to ripple, waves forming in the liquid. Impressive.

"Shh." That was enough, though. The lad needed to keep his strength up. "Now, no one expects you to do anything but heal."

The power in this one made his mouth dry as dust. Made something else hard and wet-tipped, if he was honest. He wanted to taste that power, put it under a type of control. Really, it was a weakness, this need to dominate a sweet young thing such as Paddy here. A weakness and his most beloved joy — there was nothing he enjoyed more than to see need in another's face. Need that he held the key to.

Patrick glanced at him, blue eyes clearer now. "Why are you helping me?"

"Because I wish to." Simple as that.

"Oh." As if that made perfect sense, Patrick lifted his tea, sipping as dainty as a lady.

Perhaps it did. Truths often made sense before you understood them. A man had to be open to possibilities. "Do you read, lad?"

"Yes, Sir. I had schooling."

"Good. Good. I will come and read to you." Remy kept the playing cards tucked away. Patrick was not yet well enough to play bluffs, and he wished for Patrick to be ready for his games. Many of them.

The kinds of games that left a man shaking and empty and ready for more.

"Thank you. There are no windows in this room, hmm? Is the sun still rising and falling?"

"It is. They want to make sure you have peace and quiet. I promise, you're quite safe." Poor Paddy must be worried he was a prisoner.

"I must be in a more delicate condition than I'd thought."

"You were rather torn up, *bébé*. Best to rest a while longer."

"Rest a while. Yes. Yes, I swear, I'm tired to the bone still. I don't understand it."

"That's it." The sweating would come soon. The screaming and shaking. Remy began making lists in his mind. He would need clothing. Books. Another bed set up in here. Medicine. "Come, *bébé*. Rest for me and we will start a journey together. It will be hard, but we will learn so much."

"Together?" Patrick reached out for him, eyelids drooping.

He took that large hand in his. "Yes, *bébé*. I promise."

Chapter Five

The sheets were drenched, the world a violent place filled with tremors and waves of agony. Patrick twisted, trying to drive himself up, away from the sea of bites that covered his skin. He groaned when skeletal hands reached up from the depths to pull him back down. No. He wouldn't go back.

"*Bébé. Bébé*, you are a fighter, aren't you? So strong." The voice was soft, melodic, welcome. It had a lilt to it that pleased him, soothed him.

"Sing to me?" That voice could draw him up.

"Oh, *bébé*. I haven't been asked that in a long, long time."

"Please." He couldn't see the face that went with the voice but he knew it. Hot golden brown eyes, a strong jaw, wicked mouth. Hair like a raven's wing. It made promises of things that were simply phantasms, but the sounds… Oh. The voice began to sing, a simple French lullaby, but so sweet. His tortured brain held onto the song, the melody a salve.

The grasping, bony hands clawing at him withdrew, and a kinder, warmer pair of hands began stroking his skin with a cool, wet cloth.

"It will be better soon, *bébé*. Mark my words."

"They're trying to drown me. I won't let them." Not when he could stay here. "Don't stop."

"You are safe from drowning, mark my words."

"Am I?" He laughed, but the sound was dry as dust.

"I swear to you, by all I hold holy."

Patrick opened his eyes, relieved to see the face matched his memory, blurry as it was. "You're Mister Remy."

"Very good."

"I don't feel well. I feel awful and guilty somehow." He felt as if he'd gone and done something wicked and evil.

"Guilt is not for men like us, *bébé*. Let it be gone and you will feel better." Remy stroked the cool cloth over his burning skin again.

"Is it so easy?"

"No, but then again, it doesn't need to be difficult, either." The cloth disappeared, and Remy held a glass of water to his lips. "If you practice, it becomes easier."

The cool water eased him, splashed deep in his belly. He breathed deep for the first time since he'd awakened. "Better."

"It is."

The cloths were changed, the cool rags making him gasp. He clenched and unclenched his hands, trying to adjust.

"I know, *bébé*. I went through just this before I left San Francisco. Unlike you, I did it to myself, no?"

"Why? Why would you?"

"I was feeling guilt. You see? Totally useless emotion."

"Indeed. Guilt is…" He had so many reasons for it—Henry, Caroline, his father's eternal disappointment.

"We'll work on it together. After you heal."

"Soon? How long can this linger?"

"Not long." Remy smiled, one hand resting on Patrick's chest. "Not as strong as you are."

A tingle made his muscles twitch and he pulled away from the wicked thoughts the dark hand on his chest drew forth.

"Did I hurt?" Remy asked, concern clear.

"No. No." No, that was a comfort, down deeper than skin.

"Ah, good." Remy began to hum again, that voice smoothing

over every rough nerve.

The peace made him blink, made his eyelids heavy. All he did now was sleep and dream, but he was so tired. Remy was there watching over him.

"Be at ease, *bébé*."

"You help." The words popped out, and he tried not to worry about saying them.

"Good. I want to, hmm?"

"Thank you." He blinked again and again, but couldn't focus, so he finally let his lashes fall since they were so heavy.

"Easy. Easy, *bébé*. Breathe."

"Stay with me." He shouldn't ask, but he did. He needed Remy with him.

"I have been here since the tremors began. I will remain."

"Thank you." He had no idea what he would do when he was well and Remy left him.

"Shh. I feel you."

"I didn't mean to." He hadn't tried to hurt anyone.

"I know, *bébé*. Such magnificent power. We'll teach you to control it."

Remy was so good, so incredibly dear. "My angel."

A soft chuckle followed him into his dreams. "Hardly, *lapin*. Not even close."

He didn't care what Remy said. Patrick knew an angel when he sat right there beside him.

Chapter Six

Remy lost track of the days. Poor Paddy had been deep in the lost world of laudanum, deeper than anyone Remy had ever seen. He sang until he was hoarse, changed sheets and nightshirts, and played endless rounds of solitaire.

Finally, he fell asleep, dreaming of Patrick's voice calling to him, calling him an angel.

When he woke, Patrick was bathing in the shallow tub, skin gleaming in the light of the oil lamp as he washed.

"Mmm. Did I miss dinner?" Remy asked, standing and stretching hugely.

"They brought a tray of sandwiches." Patrick offered him a shy smile. "I'm sure you could ask for something else."

"Ah, a cold collation is fine. There was a time, when I was on the trail back from San Francisco, where all I had was hard tack and pemmican. That was pure hell."

"We have lived on the same on the western front. Once, it was so desperate men killed and ate one of the horses."

Remy nodded, grimacing. "Men do things they think they are not capable of when they're fighting for their lives." He studied his Paddy with great care. "You look better."

"I feel weak as a kitten." There was a smile, though, a focus Remy hadn't seen ere now. Those blue eyes appeared clear, no confusion evident.

"I imagine so. We'll get you eating well again and that will pass."

"I needed to clean myself. I reeked."

"The sickness sweat." Remy nodded. Too bad he couldn't undress and slip into the water with Patrick. He wasn't ready for that yet. The tub wasn't either. Tiny thing.

"Yes, sir. I sweated out all the wickedness."

"That would be a real pity." He winked when Patrick's eyes widened. "But I am pleased that the crisis is over."

"I imagine so. How tiring it must be, playing nursemaid."

"I have not minded at all, *bébé*. Not one bit." He pushed some of his feeling into the words, hoping Patrick could share in it.

"Thank you. I appreciate your care, more than you know."

"Good. I might be trying to you soon." Remy advanced, grabbing a length of toweling from the stack by the tub on his way.

"Never. I am forever grateful."

"Let me help you." He would get to touch, but also cover Patrick before he lost his good sense.

"Thank you." His Paddy leaned on him as he stepped out of the tub, letting him feel that perfect weight against his side. Taller than him, Patrick would be a beautiful brute once he gained back the weight he'd lost. So much more amazing when bound and kneeling at Remy's feet then.

And the sweet, nascent cock promised to be full and swollen, begging for attention and abuse.

His body tightened, his breath catching, and he wrapped the towel around Patrick's waist. "There's still some hot water in the bucket. Do you mind if I avail myself?"

"Of course not." Patrick smiled at him, the look warm.

"Thank you." He stripped off his wrinkled blouse and undid his trouser buttons. Remy would wash in a cursory way and wait for a real bath at his house. Or perhaps upstairs.

He felt the weight of Patrick's eyes on him and he slowed his motions, allowing himself to preen a bit. He did enjoy a thorough investigation before the games began.

When he looked to Patrick, the man was flushed, eyes down.

He ducked his own head to hide a smile. "Did they bring anything besides water to drink?"

"There is more of that endless tea."

"Oh, pshaw." He hitched up his trousers and moved to the door, ready to ring for something else. Coffee. Lemonade, perhaps.

Patrick's soft laughter was welcome, warm, filled with amusement.

"I do love Anek's tea, but for God's sake, a man needs coffee. Or perhaps chocolate. Have you ever had a pot of chocolate, *bébé*?" His mother had taken a small pot every morning.

"No...I've heard of it, from other soldiers."

"I imagine you're not up to it yet, but we'll work up to it." He unlocked the door and rang for a runner.

"I've had oranges and olives, once."

"Oh, that sounds like paradise." He grinned over one shoulder. When the servant appeared, Remy turned back to the door. "Coffee, please. Do we have any pastry?"

"Of course, sir. I'll return shortly."

"Thank you." He closed and locked the door, turning to find Patrick watching him, a quizzical expression on his face. "Now, *bébé*, the shaking sickness can make a man violent. We had to be careful."

"I swear I'm in my right mind now."

"I know. We'll move to a more comfortable room very soon." He needed to test Patrick's memories again, make sure being blindsided with news of his ex-fiancée would not cause a shit storm.

"I'm not complaining. I swear to God, I'm just a bit confused."

"*Non, bébé.* I simply don't want you to worry. You're fine."

Paddy was better than fine. He was about near perfect.

Patrick smiled for him, still sitting up, color not that insipid gray from earlier days. Yes, the crisis was over, and now he could begin the training. Patrick would need what Remy gave him if he wanted to live a relatively normal life.

Otherwise he would find himself dead, or worse, in an asylum, locked away from the world. What a shame.

Remy moved to the bed, planting one hip on the mattress so he could reach out to Patrick. *Come on, bébé, take my hand.*

Patrick blinked at him, then took his hand, twining their fingers together.

"That's it." He grasped Patrick's hand warmly, rubbing his thumb over the side of Patrick's wrist.

"Have you been here long? I seem to remember you telling me about San Francisco."

"I came here nearly four years ago now, I suppose." Every time he thought about it he was shocked. He always thought of New Orleans as home, but he'd lived outside her levees for a long time.

"So, quite a while. Do you enjoy it?"

"I do. It gets cold here in the winter, which is odd." He remembered his first snow clearly. The wonder of it.

"Does it? It can be surprisingly cold out west. The wind blows and cuts through a man."

"I was lucky enough to move fast through the Western mountains on my way to California. In summer. It was bitter cold at night, though. Numbed fingers and toes, for certain." He played with Patrick's fingers, waiting for the coffee and such to arrive before becoming more serious.

"Have you seen the ocean?"

"I have. We have the bay here, lad. I'll take you soon and show you." He'd seen Campeche, the Mississippi, the vast cold oceans either side of this land. He could stand and stare at the ocean for hours given the opportunity.

The knock at the door made them both jump, and Remy chuckled when he got up to answer. "Something for us besides tea."

"Thank you." Patrick laughed. "I may not be equal to coffee, but those rolls look delicious."

They'd been sent an array of rolls and cakes, glistening with nuts and honey and cream.

"The food here is remarkable. I crave their crab cakes."

"I look forward to trying them."

"Do you? We shall have to have a feast then, once we move to a private room." Remy locked them back in and set the tray on a table before testing the waters. "What was your favorite thing to eat back home?"

"My favorite is a fried chicken with gravy. My mother's cook made that better than anyone. I miss it."

"Ah, so your *maman*, she didn't cook either?" Servants were plentiful if you could afford them.

"No. She dressed well and entertained company."

"Mine was the mistress of a very rich man." When Patrick gave him a wide-eyed look, Remy shrugged. "Beautiful woman, my *maman*. Would have been a waste for her to be poor her whole life."

He could see the confusion on Patrick's face, then the dawning of realization. "My father is a very Christian man. He allows no sinners under his roof."

"Ah. Well, I am a sinner for certain, *bébé*. I hope that sits with you."

"You are my angel."

"I've told you before, *mon coeur*, I am no *ange*."

"Still, I'm grateful for you. Honestly."

"Good." He picked up a bite-sized piece of cake, with a tiny bit of cherry preserve on it, and held it to Patrick's lips. Patrick opened up and took the bite, eyes surprised as he did.

Remy touched Patrick's lower lip gently before drawing away. "Is it good?"

"Y...yes." Sweet, innocent lad.

"I enjoy these most." He picked out a crumbly lemon shortbread and gave Patrick that next.

"Lemon!" Oh, the joy there was lovely.

"*Oui, bébé*. Like the sweets at Christmas when we were but children, no?"

"Yes. Yes, just like. Oh, now. That's fine."

"Shall we share the other? They brought us two, but I would give a bite to you." Sharing, feeding Patrick from his own hand; these things were all a good start.

"You'll spoil me like forgotten milk."

"Never. I have plans for you, Paddy. Wicked ones." Might as well be honest. Sweet Patrick would never believe it now, any road.

"Do you? Do you reckon to share?"

"My plans? Not yet. I think you're still a bit weak." He pressed the other lemon cookie to Patrick's lips before moving in quickly to take a nip of it.

Those blue eyes were huge and, for a breathtaking second, he could see it all — pain and shame, arousal and fear, a young boy beaten for sharing a kiss in a barn.

Remy reached up to stroke Patrick's stubbly cheek. "He will never harm you again, *bébé*. I swear it."

That rumble of energy came again, fighting the dampening effects of the room.

"Shh." He tested the art of distraction, leaning close again to press a gentle kiss to Patrick's lips.

"You-You know you must never do that, don't you? Someone will beat you down."

"Who will do that here? The club is very discreet about such things."

The wild-eyed confused look was at once erotic and so very regrettable. "I'm sure I don't understand."

"You will, *lapin*. I promise." He smiled. The gathering power had dissipated. His distraction had worked.

"I feel a bit like I've been in a tornado, like the world has spun."

"I imagine so. One more night in here, though, and you can move to a real room. Windows will help you regain your sense of night and day."

"I hope so. I don't quite know what to do."

"I'll help with that." Remy knew now, just knew, that Paddy would take orders beautifully. The lad would serve on hands and knees and beg for more. Oh, the things Remy had learned on the Barbary Coast in San Francisco. He wanted to teach them all to Patrick. One delicious agony at a time.

"By the time you are finished with me, I'll owe you my soul."

Remy smiled into guileless blue eyes. "I certainly hope so, *bébé*. I certainly do."

Chapter Seven

Patrick stood at attention, saluting in his nightshirt. "Lieutenant Patrick Daniels, sir, of 10 Cavalry."

"At ease, soldier." A man introduced to him only as "The Colonel" stared at him with eyes that liked to freeze him where he stood. "I have come to take stock of your condition."

"Yes, sir. Thank you, sir."

A faint smile crinkled the corners of the Colonel's eyes. "Don't thank me yet, son. You have quite a champion in Remy Blanchard. He is campaigning to move you upstairs. I am not certain you're ready."

"He has been a true gentleman and a help to me in my illness." Ready? Was he contagious?

"Remy? Are we talking about the same man?" The Colonel held up a hand to forestall his protest. "We have two main rules here. Respect the members and the staff and, while this is a club, it is a sanctuary of sorts. We don't allow nonsense and I am the law. You understand that, Lieutenant?"

"Of course, Colonel. I mean no harm."

"What you mean and what you wreak are not always the same things."

"No." His cheeks heated. Maybe this man knew all his secrets, not just some of them.

"We've got East Indians and Irish, dark folks and Injuns as servants. Can you be decent to all of them?"

"Yes, Colonel. I fought the Comanche because I was ordered to. I took no pleasure in it."

"Good man." The Colonel nodded. "Well, I'll turn you over to Remy, then. Y'all will be expected tonight at dinner with one of the other owners. A small, informal affair, so you should be up to it."

"Yes, Colonel. I-I assume that I brought an appropriate get-up with me?"

"Remy has a kit for you." The Colonel nodded again, then turned and strode to the door, knocking sharply.

"Thank you, sir." He saluted again, then dropped down on the bed as soon as the door clicked shut behind the old man. Lord have mercy, that was a bear if there ever had been one.

He looked down at his hands, which shook hard. He didn't feel sick any longer, or fuzzy in the head, but his strength was taking its own sweet time to return. He reckoned he would gain it back, with sunshine and exercise.

The door opened and stayed that way, Remy striding into the room like his very own ray of light. "You're ready, *bébé*! Shall we go explore?"

"I need trousers, Mister Remy."

"Hmm. How about a real bath, then? We'll go up the back way. There's a real bathing room up there."

"Yes, please. Please, that would be a blessing."

Remy held out a hand, his smile bright against his tanned face. He took it, feeling like he was still caught in some walking dream.

Remy pulled him out of the windowless room into what looked like a long servant's hall, then led him to a hidden set of stairs and, for a second, the room spun madly. The world itself spun madly.

Goodness, the damn place was like a maze.

"There's not an elevator. The old man didn't think it safe. You'll have to climb."

"I can. I'm strong." He had been, at any rate, once upon a time.

"Tell me if you need to catch your breath, though." Remy climbed, not stopping on the first landing.

He wouldn't. He was strong. Sure. Capable.

They climbed again and he was panting by the time they reached the third floor. Remy stopped in the hall, letting him gasp until his breathing evened. "This will be our room," Remy said, leading him to the third door down. They stepped inside, where Remy pulled the bell rope.

He leaned as casual-like as he could against the wall, not wanting to seem as worn as he was.

"We'll have a bath then a nap. I just want to make sure you have a suit of clothes pressed for supper this evening. I have some things for you, but we'll call in a tailor soon."

"Did I arrive with luggage? Saddlebags? My horse?"

"You came on the train with one valise. Your family sent a trunk on later so there are some useful things. I fear we're a tiny bit more formal here." Remy had the warmest smile. Those sherry colored eyes were so odd and wonderful.

"On the train." How had he come across the country and not remembered it?

"Yes. There were a few areas where you traveled by coach, but mostly by train." Remy glided close, resting a hand on his chest. "You had quite a trip."

He sucked in a breath, a worried panic filling him. "I reckon I don't remember. I don't remember a bit."

His folks wouldn't have sent him alone, would they?

"Hush. Your heart is pounding like a hammer. You came with a dear friend of mine. He's also a friend of your father's man, Jedidiah."

That name was familiar to him, and he found a measure of peace in it. Jedidiah was a good man, not one to blindly follow orders.

"Better?"

"Yes. May I sit?"

"Of course, *bébé*. You must always tell me what you need."

"I'm a little lost." He headed toward the window, sitting where he could stare out.

"Are you?" Remy followed him, standing with one hand on his shoulder.

"Yes, sir, I reckon I am." A little lost and more than a touch confused.

"I am not worried." Remy began to rub the back of his neck, the touch so gentle, but firm enough to ease his muscles. The touch made his eyelids heavy, made his breath catch in his chest. He felt… Well, his heart thundered, but his tension melted. How was that possible?

"You're fine, *bébé*. Breathe."

"I'm trying." He chuckled, not at all sure if he should be nervous or excited. He looked around the room, surprised to find an apartment of sorts, a door leading to a bedchamber, another to a bathing room. How decadent.

"It is a lovely place," Remy agreed. "Would you like a real bath? There's a boiler so we have running water."

"That sounds heavenly." He nodded, eager. He wanted a real cleaning, with soap and water. Maybe he could trim his hair. Remy had been faithful about cleaning up his face, but he could do it with a razor and a bit of looking glass.

"Come along, then." Remy helped him rise once more, leading him to the bathing room. A high rimmed tub sat inside, the floor tiled in an Egyptian palm frond pattern. The water began to flow under Remy's hand, and then Remy turned to him to begin unbuttoning his nightshirt.

He stared, the dark skin so fine against the cotton lawn. Patrick knew he was no child who needed a nanny to bathe him, but Remy did not make him feel like a child. Not in the least. In fact, Remy made him ache in ways that might see him burn in hellfire.

"There you are." Remy tugged off his nightshirt, then guided him into the water, which felt so good lapping at his calves.

"Thank you. Goodness, it's warm. Nice."

"It is, hmm? There's some lovely sandalwood soap." Remy knelt by the tub, then grabbed a pot of soap from a stand beside him.

The scent was heady, and he breathed it deep, luxuriating in it. Stimulating.

Remy dipped a cloth into the water before lathering up the soap. Then he began to wash Patrick, beginning at the collarbones.

"I—" He blinked, suddenly unsure. "I should—"

"Relax and let me help you." Remy stared into his eyes, hand moving on his chest, the cloth abrasive enough to make his nipples rise into hard points.

He willed himself not to moan, not to close his eyes and whimper. Sin. This was a sin. His body loved sin, and he glanced down to see if his shaft had betrayed him by rising above the waterline.

His eyes flashed open wide, and his hands dropped down over his erection, hiding his shame. "Perhaps I should, um, the rag, please?"

"No, *bébé*. I am giving you a bath. Take your hand away." Remy scrubbed his belly, the cloth catching the fine hairs there.

"But, you cain't— I'm—" Hard. He was aching with it.

"Yes, you are." The cloth brushed the back of his hand. "Lovely."

"Forgive me. I've been ill."

"I know. The only thing to forgive is that we could not do this sooner because of it. Now, lift your hand." That caramel voice held a note of command, as if Remy was an officer, commanding him to come to attention.

His hands lifted as if he had no will of his own, his eyes

pulling at the corners.

"That's it, Patrick." Remy dipped the cloth below water, stroking the length of his cock. Measuring him.

"You cannot." He stared, his entire body going taut as frozen rope.

"I can and I will, *bébé*. Further, you want me to." Remy was relentless.

It was a sin, but his body cared not a whit, his cock throbbed, hard and needy. He'd never felt anything so scandalous in his life, Remy rubbing up and down, up and down, slow and easy.

The water began to shudder, to splash against the sides of the tub, faster and harder.

"Shh." Remy gripped the base of his cock, shocking him into stillness. "Look at me, Patrick. Right into my eyes."

He met Remy's dark gaze, the expression near mesmerizing. Patrick fell into Remy rather like falling in a well, his breath catching, his chest heaving.

"*Oui*. That's it. Only me, *bébé*. Focus on me. All is well."

He opened his mouth to argue, but not a single word popped out. He could only nod and watch Remy's face when that hand began to move again, sliding down his cock to the base, then beneath to scrub his balls.

Please.

He had no idea whether he begged for Remy to continue or to cease. None. He simply begged wordlessly for assistance.

"I won't let you fall." Remy leaned over the side of the tub, lips touching his in a strangely chaste kiss, considering the motions of his hand.

The touch of those lips seemed to still the quaking deep inside his brain. He held his hands against his chest, but he began to rock his hips, asking for more of that unnerving addiction. The water rushed past his sac, his backside slipping in the tub.

"Easy," Remy said against his mouth. "We're in no hurry."

"We're being wicked. Awful bad."

"We're enjoying a simple touch, *lapin*." Remy made it so reasonable.

"Simple." There hadn't been anything simple feeling about this.

"Yes. There's no shame here. Only need. I can give you what you need." Remy kissed just under his ear, drawing a shiver.

What he needed. Another rumble deep inside him began to build, to shake.

Remy pressed up under his balls, derailing every thought in his mind. He lost track of all the pieces of his soul, his body overriding everything.

"Only me, *bébé*. Only my will."

He didn't understand, but he found he didn't have to. He just had to spread his legs and arch up, his toes curled, thighs shaking.

"Such a good boy. A natural, hmm?" The musical voice just kept going, spinning around him like Remy was casting a spell.

"Natural."

"*Oui*. You see. You begin to comprehend." The cloth rubbed farther, down to his most private place.

The water made a whirlpool, a wild eddy around his body.

"So expressive. I can see what a challenge you'll be." Remy backed away, the cloth sliding back up his cock.

"I don't understand." And the trying to made the bridge of his nose hurt.

"You will. I vow it, Paddy. But you don't need to right now." The water calmed again, Remy's motions slower, more measured.

He felt a little like a child dropped in a maelstrom, but then the touches to his body weren't anything like a child's. Not a bit. Remy was a man's man who knew what he was about. Confident. Patrick had to wonder, briefly, where Remy had learned this. Then he forgot how to think again because Remy's lips latched onto his neck, sucking up what had to be a mark on his skin.

His eyes crossed and his hands patted on the water, restless. "You cain't."

"No one will see but me." Remy bit, worrying that piece of skin.

It would be worse, if it hadn't felt so good. As it was, Patrick found himself willing to understand Remy's words, to believe.

That hand slid up and down, up and down, relentless, until the cloth slipped away, nothing between their skin but water.

"Please." He had not one idea what he begged for—but he believed that Remy would offer it to him somehow.

"Soon, *bébé*. Soon. You smell so good now. All clean male musk. I want to explore every inch of you with my hands. My mouth. I want to see you spread and begging for me. Only me."

His eyes went wide, the words beyond imagining, beyond belief. He gaped, his ass cheeks clenching, his cock rising high out of the water as he spent his seed, his ears ringing with the force of it.

"Oh, lovely." Remy's voice was like silk against him.

"Oh, God in heaven. I'm sorry. That bathwater."

"Shh… I didn't need to share it." Remy stroked him until his cock felt almost sore, then patted it gently. "Soon you'll learn to please me, too, but for now you need to rest up for your meeting with Jules, hmm?"

Remy stood him up on trembling legs and led him from the bath to a clean, quiet bedchamber. He was eased down on the deep feather bed, Remy smoothing down the sheets before covering him with them.

He didn't know what to say, not in the least. So he lay there, with his eyes closed.

"Julian will expect us later. One of the servants will alert us a half hour before."

He heard the rustle of fabric before Remy slipped under the

sheets with him. One arm fell across his waist, as bare as he was. His instinct was to stiffen, but his body melted, relaxed. Eased into the ticking.

The warmth of Remy against his side was right. Wonderful.

"Be at ease, *bébé*. All is well."

"Thank you." What else could he say? Nothing, so he slept.

Chapter Eight

The soft knock on the door brought Remy awake, and he rolled from the bed to go and accept the pressed clothing the servant handed him.

"Half an hour, sir," the fellow said.

"*Merci.*" He hung the clothes on the wardrobe before returning to Patrick. "Wake up, *bébé.*"

The sweet eyes opened slowly, gaze meeting his. So blue. Like wildflowers or the Texas sky. Remy smiled at his flight of fancy. "Supper is nearly upon us."

"We meet the head man here, you said. Not the Colonel."

"There's more than one head man, but yes. Julian is charming. English. Quite lovely. He only wants to meet you."

"I'll mind my manners, you have my word."

"I am certain." Remy stood naked next to the bed, hands on his hips. Patrick obviously didn't want to look, but he was peeking, the golden lashes fluttering as he was admired. He let the lad stare. He cut a fine figure and he knew it.

Then he scratched his belly, humming. "They pressed you a suit of clothes."

"Thank you." Patrick stood, the muscled body too lean, but still fine, proving years of hard work, which was odd for a wealthy man. Then again, he'd been a younger son and a soldier.

Remy had to touch. He stepped close, one hand on Patrick's hip.

Those sapphire chip eyes flashed to him, wide and surprised, shocked.

That was an expression Remy looked forward to provoking over and over. "If we had time, *lapin*, I would suck your cock until you screamed. We shall save it for later."

Sweet lips opened and closed, again and again, a bit like a landed fish gasping to survive.

He patted Paddy's taut ass smartly. "Dress. We don't want to be late."

"No. No, I don't reckon. Lord. The things you say."

"You like them." Remy pulled on his trousers and shirt, pushing the collar into place and fastening it on.

Patrick went to the suit and dressed himself in the fine clothes, looking a bit odd all done up and covered up. Remy was now quite used to having as much access as he wished.

"I usually wear my uniform for formal occasions. Well, I did before I mustered out."

"I imagine you cut a fine figure." He moved back across the room to straighten Patrick's tie.

When he opened the door, the same servant waited to guide them to another third-floor room, a private meeting space that had been set with a dining table and chairs.

"Ah, Remy." Julian rose from the table, where he'd been lounging rather than sitting. "And this must be Patrick Daniels. I am Julian Fitzhugh."

Julian held out a strong, square hand that seemed at odds with his silver gilt coloring. Pale blond hair and silver gray eyes were striking against the black evening kit.

"Pleased to make your acquaintance, sir." Paddy shook hands, dipped his chin, the slow drawl pronounced. "I appreciate your hospitality while I was indisposed and all."

"You are most welcome." Julian's clipped, English accent was a stark contrast. So very civil. "Our good friend Canaan vouched for you. Frankly, though, Remy's interest in you piqued mine. Please, sit. I ordered a rather bland menu, as I understand you're still recovering."

Patrick sat, but the confusion was writ plain on the dear face, and the china rattled, just a bit.

Julian sank into his chair, and Remy smiled at him, knowing the best way to assess a potential threat was to keep said threat off guard.

Patrick had great power, but Remy was confident it could be controlled. He'd seen a whisper of it and, more than that, he'd seen how well Patrick responded to command.

"I guess that means no gumbo, hey?" Remy pouted, knowing Julian would laugh for him.

"No, though there is a soup course. Then roasted fowl and dressing."

"Mmm. I do admit that I miss my tasso when I am here. Are you a fan of spicy food, Julian my dear?" He lived to tease.

"I prefer mild spice in my food. What about you, Patrick?"

"I'm a simple man and a soldier, I reckon. I like to eat."

"Good, good." Julian waved a hand, and a server appeared. "Milk? We also have coffee and wine."

"I would appreciate milk, if you don't mind."

No, Remy didn't imagine Patrick's constitution was ready for wine.

"Coffee for you, Remy?" Julian asked.

Only Remy knew it was more than a suggestion. He nodded. "As long as there's sugar."

"Addict." Julian nodded to the server. "And wine for me, if you please."

"Of course, sir. Right away."

Patrick looked about the room, at the fine china with a pattern of tiny snowdrops with delicate green ivy. Remy could see his discomfiture, the way he shifted in his chair.

"Tell me about Texas," Julian demanded. "I have never been there."

"It's vast, sir. I live in the land of cotton, but I served out in the Indian territories, in the badlands. Where my father lives, it is green, lush."

"Are there mountains?" Being the focus of all of Julian's attention could be unnerving. Remy wasn't entirely sure what Julian might be capable of, but he knew there was a keen mind behind those silver eyes.

"They say so, near Austin, but I haven't seen them with my eyes. The badlands have crags and valleys like nothing I'd ever seen before."

"It sounds a fascinating place. I come from someplace wet and green. So green it can hurt your eyes." Julian glanced at Remy. "Then there's our man from the swamps."

"Oh, *cher*, I love me some Spanish moss and alligators."

"I have never traveled east before now. I don't remember the trip here at all."

"Maybe someday we'll go and see," Remy murmured.

"Someday," Julian agreed, watching Patrick closely. "Not today."

No. No, his dear Patrick may never be safe to travel again, not the way the plates clattered against the chargers. Remy reached out and put a hand over Patrick's. The rattle stopped abruptly, and Julian smiled, the look vaguely like one of the gators he'd grown up with.

"I hope you continue to grace us with your presence, Patrick, at least for a bit. You'll find the Raven a generous, welcoming club."

"Thank you." Patrick was beginning to look like a fractious pony, too much eye white showing, when the first course arrived. Who could resist a velvety soup with chicken and vegetables?

Patrick's nostril flared and the soup spun in the bowl, but only for a second, fast enough it might have been a trick of the ladle.

"Shall I dish out?" Remy asked. They were going casual,

really, with only the one server.

"Please." Julian waved a hand and the ladle clanked over to his side of the bowl.

He chuckled softly and took it. Mimicry was the most genuine form of flattery, after all. Julian was exceptional at it, from vocal impressions to mental talents. Such a mockingbird. Julian stuck his tongue out at him, and Remy laughed, the visual of the staid Brit dissolving with the singular expression. Even Patrick relaxed enough to laugh. The soup smelled even better out of the tureen, and the crusty bread accompanying it made a meal of itself.

Patrick ate well, if slowly, obviously enjoying the meal. Remy had to admit, the roasted duck and dressing filled him to the brim, and he groaned when the trifle was presented.

"Never fear, Remy. I ate sparingly of supper so I could enjoy dessert." Julian laughed and dug deep into the fruit and custard concoction.

Patrick took a bare spoonful, then pushed it away.

Remy looked Patrick over carefully, to decide if he was simply tired or if he hated trifle. Perhaps it was a bit of both.

"Apologies. I'm stuffed to the gills."

"Nothing to worry on. I know a good many club members who will help."

"Excellent. Wastefulness is a sin."

Julian exchanged a glance with Remy. "Sometimes sin is good, but not in this case."

"Sin is a pointless regret," Remy growled.

"Spoken like a true son of the Catholic church, Remy."

"Bah." Remy flipped a hand languidly. "Saints are just a cover for the vodoun."

"Vodoun?" Sweet innocent boy.

"The gods of voodoo, sweet boy," Julian said. "Fascinating nature religion."

"Voodoo. That sounds like a song."

Remy hummed. "Oh, it is, *bébé*. A glorious pagan song with a deep soul."

Patrick looked at him, dazed, fascinated.

Julian chuckled, licking his spoon. "Such a sybarite, our Remy."

"He is my angel." The simple words settled deep in Remy's heart.

"A fallen one?" Julian asked.

Patrick shrugged, hands spread wide. "What does that matter, so long as he is here?"

"That is most true, Patrick." Julian nodded easily, as if he'd made up his mind about Patrick Daniels. Remy was relieved.

They chatted a bit longer, and Patrick began to droop. "I think it's time Patrick rested," Remy said.

"Mmm. Come have a nightcap with me later," Julian said. It was not a request.

"I'll be back shortly."

"I'll look forward to it."

Remy rose, holding out a hand to Patrick, and his lad took it, blinking up at him in an exhausted daze.

Poor sweet *bébé*. Remy nodded at Julian before leading him out of the room. "Overdid it, I think. Sorry, sweet. Julian is a bad influence."

"No. No, I ought to be able to survive a supper."

"You will, I promise. You're doing so well."

"You flatter me." Patrick offered him a smile, the barest touch to his wrist.

The contact gave him a shiver. They definitely progressed.

"That was forward of me, I beg your pardon."

"No need." He took Patrick's hand and they made their way back to the room they had been assigned. "Julian will expect me back soon. I think he gets lonely."

"I can manage my clothing, my friend."

"I know you can, but it pleases me to help." He wanted the stimulation of seeing Patrick nude before him again.

Patrick's cheeks pinked, his head ducking with his pleasure.

Smiling, Remy began by divesting Patrick of his coat, then his waistcoat and tie. Patrick didn't fight him, watching him with near drugged eyes.

He kissed a spot of bare skin before dropping to his knees to remove the soft shoes Patrick wore, then the trousers.

"You...you're lovely."

"No, *lapin*. You're the pretty one." He smoothed down the trousers before rubbing his cheek against Paddy's cock, partly covered by the lawn shirt he still wore.

Patrick drew in a desperate breath, filling his lungs with a hiss.

So responsive. The perfect lover for Remy and he knew it. He licked at the tip, then gave Patrick's balls a gentle tug before rising. "Promise me you'll stay here and rest. I will return soon."

"You have my word." Paddy swayed, hips bucking for him, rolling that heavy cock.

He slapped it lightly with the palm of his hand. "No touching yourself. That is for me." Remy turned on his heel and left before he forgot to go.

He could hear the low groan as he closed the door behind him.

Ruefully, Remy glanced down at his own hard cock, which pressed against his buttons. He rapped on the door to the room where Julian waited.

"Come in, my dear." Julian's voice was like silk.

"Are you well, *mon ami*?" It never hurt to gauge Julian's mood.

"I am. Come sit and tell me about your find."

Remy strode into the room so he might throw himself into a chair across from Julian. "He is endlessly fascinating."

"Is he aware of his gift?"

Remy snorted softly. "He is an innocent in so many senses of the word."

"So, no. You seem to have him well in hand already." Julian tapped a finger on the table.

"I have high hopes to, yes. He needs to explore the limits of control."

"The mind boggles." Julian glanced pointedly at his fly. "I haven't seen you so excited since I've known you."

"I haven't had an opportunity like this. He...I find him fascinating."

"Hmm." Julian smiled, then stood to grab a crystal decanter to pour them a drink. "Just be sure he is under control and that it's not an illusion, my friend."

"Julian." He blinked over, letting his inner gator show a bit. "I assure you, I understand illusions."

"Mmm." Julian laughed. "I do adore you. If he's powerful, however, I have a vested interest in him not letting loose here, and you know it."

"Of course. That is why he's here, after all, is it not?"

"Of course." Julian handed him a glass of brandy.

"*Merci.* Now tell me, what is your worry? Let me ease you."

"You mean aside from your Texan?" Julian smiled. "You know me too well."

That was, after all, why he was here.

Chapter Nine

Patrick slept hard, dreaming of a certain dark-eyed angel who tempted him, who promised wickedness. In his dreams, Remy came to him naked, that brown body shining with sweat, magnificently hard and ready. Shameful, that need.

He moaned and leaned down, daring to drag his tongue over the fine skin, gathering up the salt that he found there. Oh, dear God in heaven, he wanted more. How did he get what he needed?

You cannot! A line of fire slashed across his back, shoulder to hip, and he roared, the world going fiery for a moment.

Another lash fell, then another, and he screamed out his rage and pain. Patrick knew he was a sinner, but this was hellfire on earth.

"Patrick! *Bébé*, wake up!" Someone was shaking him hard enough his teeth rattled.

His eyes popped open and he flew from the bed, his back slamming against the wall, his breath huffing from him.

The washbasin settled back on its stand, the pitcher crashing to the floor, water sloshing.

Remy stared at him from where he stood next to the bed. "You were dreaming."

"I'm sorry. Please, forgive me." He shook his head, trying to clear it.

Holding out a hand, Remy smiled gently. "Must have been a hell of a dream."

"Yessir." He stood up, straightening his soaking wet nightshirt.

"Oh, *lapin*, let's take that off."

"Is there another?"

"You won't need one." Remy came to him, bending to lift the hem of his shirt up.

"Pardon?" He was shaking with sweat.

"You can sleep without it. You'll be cooler. Arms up."

He blinked and lifted his arms. "I'm sorry that I woke you."

"You didn't. I was still talking with Julian until a few moments ago."

"Ah. Good. Good." He took the discarded gown and wiped his face off, his shoulders and back screaming. Or did they scream? Was it real?

"Are you hurting?" Remy took his shirt and set it aside.

"I—" Was he? "Just the dream."

"Mmm. I can make that better." Remy caressed his hip before beginning to strip off his evening kit.

He doubted that. That had been Satan scolding him. Satan in the form of...His mind skittered from the thought.

"Shh." Remy stopped with shirt and trousers still on. "I should not have left you alone so long." Then Remy embraced him, the touch shocking and intimate.

"Men do not…" But it felt right, a comfort deep inside.

"Why not? Because someone said so when you were young? Because some deacon preached hellfire? Bah."

That sound made him snort, made him chuckle.

Remy grabbed his butt with both hands. Squeezed. "There, now. That's better."

"Forgive me. Demons must have found me asleep."

"They do find us at the strangest time. Help me with my clothing?"

"Of course." He could play manservant. He undid the tiny

pearl buttons on Remy's blouse, trying not to think of what he was doing. The scent of Remy filled his nose, rich and spicy and unique.

Remy kissed him as a reward.

He stood there, trembling for a moment before he stepped back. "We cannot. It's a sin."

Remy stared at him a moment, then nodded easily. "Very well, *lapin*. I'll sleep on the cot." Remy stepped out of his boots and shucked his trousers. He turned his back to Patrick to bend over and remove the cloth, his ass round and firm, the shadow of his balls just there.

"No. No. That is unkind and... Please. Please, take the bed. I didn't mean to be...I dreamed—Take the bed."

"We can share it, *bébé*." Remy turned back to face him. "Tell me what you dreamed. We can face it together."

"I—" His face burned and thank God it was dark, because damnation, he couldn't meet Remy's eyes. "I dreamed I was being wicked and then a devil came to beat on me."

"Ah." Remy smiled, but there was nothing in it but kindness. "I told you, worry over sin is overrated. Come sit with me."

They sank down on the edge of the bed, Remy holding his hand.

"It's like the world is different now. Has been since…" The bed rattled gently beneath them.

"Mmm. I imagine so. I know it's quite a bit to take in." Remy half turned to face him, hand coming up to rest over his thundering heart. "I'm here to help."

He wasn't so sure about that. Remy seemed to make his need that much worse.

"Do you trust me?" Remy asked, fingers moving gently on Patrick's chest.

Remy was his angel, his touchstone in a world gone odd. "I do."

"Then trust me to make the demons go away." Remy kissed his mouth, a sweet touch of lips he barely had time to brace for. The caress made him sigh, the touch a comfort.

Pushing gently, Remy lowered him to the mattress, a down-filled wonder. That lean, hard body molded to his, one arm over his belly. "Rest now, *lapin*. The next lesson can wait."

"Take care of yourself. I can struggle in my dreams."

"I'm right here." Remy patted his chest. "We can do it together."

He grunted, sleep weighing him like a blanket. The demons would have to work hard to wake him, as tired as he was.

Mayhap this time, Remy would guard his dreams instead of allowing the devil in.

He would believe it and it would be true. It had to be.

Chapter Ten

Remy bided his time.

Patience was one of his strong suits, though most people would never believe it. Like an alligator in a Louisiana swamp, he was an ambush predator, waiting for his chance to strike, whether in cards or in love.

Oh. Cards.

He rose from his seat in the large leather chair he had brought to Patrick's bedchamber. "Do you play bluffs?" he asked.

Patrick chuckled softly. "I admit I have, yes, although I would admit it to no one but you."

"No?" He smiled. So worried about being sinful, his *bébé*. "I love cards."

"My brother Henry and I played often."

"Does it make you sad to think of him?" Remy asked, watching carefully. It would be valuable to know what set off his new lover.

Patrick reached up and stroked the back of his head. "He's distant and constant, all at once. For sharing a womb, we were different as night and day."

"Tell me about him?" Remy moved to rummage through his valise for a pack of cards.

"He was built for business. A leader of men. A good son. I am less so, on every count."

"What is your best skill, then?" He sat across from Patrick at the little table they used for some of their meals and began to shuffle.

"I like to ride."

"So were you a good cavalry man? All day in the saddle?" He wanted to see Patrick ride him at some point.

"I like to think so. I can shoot and ride. I was a good soldier. At least until I was wounded."

"What happened?" Remy was intensely curious about everything.

"My brother was killed, shot through the heart."

The answer wasn't to the question he asked.

"What happened to you, though?" He dealt a five card hand.

"My brother was shot."

How very odd. Remy tilted his head, wondering who he could call upon at the Raven to look into this. Some of the members could see into other's heads.

Patrick took the cards as if he'd answered the question perfectly.

Remy allowed it to drop for now. He looked at his cards. Oh, that was a whole lot of nothing.

Patrick smiled softly, the expression pleased, but not excited. No mistaking what Patrick might have. He would never ask Patrick to play against, say, Canaan.

That little ball of evil was a challenge and would steal his boy's soul.

He waited for Patrick to bid, then bid on nothing, really, needing the draw.

Patrick took a single card.

Remy took three. He wondered what to play for after this hand. He hadn't asked for any kind of ante.

Perhaps he should ask for kisses, information, something to push his dear innocent. He wondered what would rattle in the room if he asked Paddy to kiss his cock.

He might have to put Patrick in the windowless room for that.

Patrick called and won the hand, and Remy raised an eyebrow. "What shall we play for now, *lapin*?"

"I used to play for tobacco and coin, but I have neither."

"Mmm. I could loan you money. Or we could play for kisses."

"Kisses?" Patrick laughed for him, the sound soft, husky. "That sounds dangerous."

"Life should be fraught with danger. Makes it more interesting. Say yes."

"What has a kiss ever hurt, hmm?"

"Precisely. We'll ante up with one."

"Sounds fair enough."

It was more than fair, because he intended to win this hand. And the next.

It was less than fair, but this was not about reason, this was about need.

He offered the cards to Patrick. "Would you like to deal?"

"Surely. Thank you." Patrick shuffled carefully, then offered him the deck to cut.

Remy cut, willing the cards to do his bidding.

He was handed a three of a kind. What a very good boy. "I'll bid one kiss, *bébé*."

"One kiss." Patrick read his cards. "Yes. All right. I will see your kiss."

"I'll take two cards." Might as well try for a full house or four of a kind.

"Yessir." Patrick dealt, and took three for himself.

Interesting. He studied his cards. Still three of a kind but he would bet the hand was his. "I will see your kiss and raise two."

"That's...that's three, then?" Such delicious need. The tremor in Paddy's fingers, the way he licked his lips, they told Remy how much Patrick wanted him.

"That's three."

"I will meet your bet."

"I will call, then."

"I have two pairs." Patrick smiled over, pleased.

"Very nice." Remy spread out his cards on the table. "Three of a kind."

Patrick's eyes went wide, then he grinned sheepishly. "I thought I had a good chance."

"You did. We both win, though, since we wanted the same thing. With the ante, that's four kisses you owe me."

"I...Do you wish them all at once?"

"We'll begin with one." He smiled, eager to taste a kiss freely given, not stolen.

Patrick leaned over, breath soft where it brushed against his lips. Remy let Patrick come all the way to him, the kiss soft and sweet, gentle and careful.

When it ended, Remy sighed softly. "*Oui, bébé.* Again."

"Again." This kiss was the same, but the pressure of one of Patrick's hands settled on his thigh.

Remy reached up to slide his fingers into Patrick's thick hair, and he gently tilted Patrick's head, deepening their connection.

Patrick moaned into his lips, leaning harder against his leg, seeking more. He pushed a bit with his tongue, letting Patrick feel his eagerness. And they had two kisses left for this hand.

Patrick's lips opened on a gasp, a sweet little intake of air.

Remy hummed, a happy sound, and let his fingers play against Patrick's nape, the spot warm and tender. The bed shuddered, the creak as it slipped across the floor a bare warning.

Pulling back slightly, Remy smiled. "Pay attention, *mon doux.* Just me. You and me and kisses."

"I am. We have two left."

"We do. I think I want them now." He scooted around the table a bit so they were even closer together. If there was a lesson to be taught here, he intended to be close enough to teach it.

Paddy closed his eyes, golden lashes heavy on his cheeks. He gave the next kiss even more easily, lips warm now. Damp.

He moaned softly and let one hand land on Patrick's belly.

Patrick jumped slightly, his breath coming faster every second. A small sound vibrated against his lips, a tiny moan of pleasure, he thought. Then another kiss, this one harder, edged with need and teeth, that only lasted seconds before Patrick pulled away.

Patrick stared at him, blue eyes wide. "Remy."

"There's nothing to be afraid of."

"I ain't afraid." Such pride.

"I know. You do worry too much about sin."

"You don't fear for your soul?"

"No, *bébé*. I told you. That's a futile thing." Remy shrugged. "If there is a hell as your people believe, then I suppose I will go there, but I am not afraid."

"Then I reckon I won't either." The stubborn set of Patrick's jaw made him smile.

"Good. One more kiss then, before we play another hand?" He loved kissing. Patrick had surprisingly rough stubble for such a fair man, stinging Remy's skin.

"Yes. I believe one more." Patrick leaned in, sharing their air a moment.

Remy took this kiss instead of simply accepting it, holding Patrick there with him, hand behind Patrick's hair. The bed slid across the floor as Patrick opened to him.

He used his other hand to pinch Patrick's nipple, distracting him. Those bright blue eyes went wide, staring into him.

"When you feel overwhelmed, *bébé*, give that to me. Do you hear?"

"I don't understand."

"You don't have to. You only have to listen. Give it to me. Only me."

"Only you."

He nodded. He found himself quite possessive of all of Patrick's energies. He wanted everything.

"More games, *lapin*, or would you like to go explore together in that slippery bed?"

Patrick's mouth opened and closed, then his hand was taken like Patrick had no words left to him.

Remy took him to bed. Now. He had to move now.

His prick was full and aching, his body screaming to plaster itself to Patrick's. Remy stripped them both out of the few clothes they had assumed for the day, then pressed Patrick down and back.

Patrick's eyes were fastened to his, watching him like a hawk. Yes. That was the focus he needed. He kissed Patrick hard and deep, rewarding the lad for his obedience, intent on taking what he required so desperately.

The room stayed still, the only motion that of their bodies on the bed. All of Patrick's enormous energy poured into Remy, and it was better than anything voodoo could conjure.

"Good boy. Good. Just so." He nuzzled in, biting at Patrick's lips.

"Remy." Patrick huffed out a tiny laugh. The idea of being a good boy seemed to mystify him.

Patrick moaned for him, long body undulating. Remy slid one hand down over Patrick's chest and belly, exploring, smiling at the instinctive motions his *bébé* made. The long cock was hard and curved, tapping the muscled belly. He had to measure it with his hand before tugging at it.

"Remy." The sound of his name in Patrick's voice was like a prayer.

"Yes, *lapin*. Your cock is so hard."

"Should I be sorry?"

"Never. I want to taste it. Touch it."

Paddy stared at him, wide-eyed, shock like a physical thing.

Nothing in the room crashed or moved, however, so Remy called that a win.

He petted Patrick's thighs. "I could spend days worshipping you. With my hands. My mouth."

"No one's ever said such things…"

"No? You've been in too polite company. I knew a Creole woman in New Orleans who could make her men come just talking to them. She had a voice, that one."

Patrick dropped his voice. "There was a woman — someone my father took me to, but I paid her to tell him I performed."

"Mmm. I can see that. I have never gone that route myself. This woman was a friend of my mother's." He fingered Patrick's cock, just dancing over the flared head. "I fear I do have more experience than you with the male of the species."

"I reckon you got more experience than me with damn near everything but horses and screwing up."

"Oh, now, I am a disappointment to many, *mon doux*." He leaned close to lick away a drop of sweat beading on Patrick's collarbone.

"No…" Patrick arched beautifully, column of throat working as he lingered.

"Indeed. My *maman* wanted me to marry and produce dozens of wee ones. My white, plantation owning father wished me to fight for the South."

"And here you are. My angel."

"I am meant for you, *bébé*." He meant it, too. He found himself more and more convinced of that fact, every day.

Paddy beamed for him, cheeks pink. "May I touch you, too?"

Such pretty manners. "Of course."

Patrick drew lazy patterns over his chest, the touch stuttering only the barest bit. Hesitant but curious. The best kind of lover, because he would take direction.

"Lower, *bébé*." He wanted those trembling fingers around his need.

Patrick's blue gaze flashed to his. That lower lip pushed out, Patrick's chin setting with determination. He fought his urge to crow, needing to allow Patrick this little victory.

Those long, callused fingers wrapped around his prick, Patrick's grip firm, if inexpert. His *bébé* gasped, eyes rolling and the bed shifted once more.

"No. No, right here. Watch me."

Patrick's eyes flew open. "Remy."

"Just watch me, Paddy. Only me." He arched, pushing into Patrick's fist.

"Only…" Patrick squeezed his fingers, gripping him.

Remy nodded hard, his breath coming fast. "You please me so much."

"I want to. You've offered me so much."

"Have I?" He'd locked Patrick away and kept him isolated, but that was better than an asylum, or worse, killing him as Matthias had wished to.

"Yessir." Patrick stole another kiss, this one edged with need.

Remy took the kiss deeper than ever before, pushing Patrick to really feel his intent, and Patrick opened to him, tongue sliding against his own. They rolled a bit on the bed until they were side by side, able to explore, to touch. Their erections brushed together, and the sound that simple touch drew from Patrick was a siren song.

So Remy did it again, then again. He rubbed them together as if he might start a fire with two sticks. That image was not so far off. He felt like he might catch flame, just light up in a blaze.

Patrick was right with him, moaning and rubbing, but as long as those bright blue eyes stayed on him, nothing in the room moved but them.

That's right. Offer all that need to me, all that passion. Remy thought it hard, intent on keeping Patrick focused. Ready. Needing him like no one else ever had.

Remy found a tiny patch of skin to bite on Patrick's shoulder, knowing the sting would make his boy dance for him, ache just that much more. He would leave his marks on Patrick's soul.

Patrick jerked, cock leaving a wet trail against Remy's skin.

He dragged his fingers through the slick drops, then brought them to his lips, tasting his *bébé*'s seed.

"Oh, dear Lord." Patrick kissed him, just clumsy and near brutal. The bureau drawers flew open, clothes filling the air.

Remy reached down, tugging Patrick's balls down away from his cock. "Breathe. Focus. Me."

"I am!" The looking glass rattled.

"Harder. Look into me, *bébé*."

Patrick met his gaze. "What's wrong with me?"

"Nothing, *lapin*." He stroked that cock fast, keeping it hard. "You have an amazing natural talent. God given, you would say. We just need to help you control it."

"You swear it? You swear I ain't broke?"

"I swear." No. No, while this very well may have resulted from an injury, Patrick was certainly not broken.

"All right then." Patrick eased, and so did the trembling of the room.

"That's what I want to do, besides make love with you. I want to help."

"Why? What do you get from it?" Those eyes watched him, an agony of confusion in them.

"You." Remy stopped the whole world to say the words. "I get you, heart and soul and body, Patrick."

"I hope you don't regret it."

"Never." He smiled, knowing the alligator spirit was probably showing through. Patrick never seemed to fear him.

In fact, that made Patrick's blue eyes darken and their lips came together again. He never let go of his prize, and Remy set about stroking hard, really making Patrick feel him. Patrick's hand answered his, the caresses making his balls draw up.

Remy grunted, his belly drawing in, his need exploding at the base of his spine. "Soon."

"You need." Patrick bit his bottom lip.

"I want you with me, *bébé*," he demanded. "I want to see and feel it."

He made sure to punctuate his words with a hard stroke to the tip of Patrick's need.

Patrick arched up and back, tendons standing out in his neck. "Uhn!"

"*Oui*. Just so." He repeated the motion and Patrick squeezed ever tighter.

Remy moaned, his body giving it up, so he slapped Patrick's cock with the flat of his hand, wanting them to arrive as one.

The scent of them together made him moan, made his mouth water. He kept stroking until he thought Patrick had given every drop. Then he brought his slick fingers to his mouth.

Patrick joined him this time, licking at the seed Remy had left on Patrick's hand.

"*Mon doux*. So sweet. You're learning to need, *oui*?"

"Learning. You make me want things, Remy."

"I can't wait to explore them." The things he wished to explore would make his innocent shudder, split his beliefs down the middle.

Remy laughed for the sheer joy of that idea. Patrick had spent himself and nothing in the room had even creaked. Now it was time to begin training in earnest. They would start with dinner in the private member area, maybe tomorrow.

"What's funny?" So curious, his Paddy.

"Nothing, really. I'm simply very happy to be with you." He could devote his life to it, in fact.

Patrick's cheeks went a bright, rosy red and his lover ducked his chin, obviously pleased.

Remy stroked Patrick's hair back off his forehead. Yes, he could do this forever. Well, hopefully at home, eventually.

His staff would be so pleased — the rag-tag group of Islanders and pirates were led by his man, Jean, and they were wicked and wild to a person. They would love corrupting Patrick with the pleasures of food and drink and cards… He'd have to make sure they had a place nearby to stable horses. Remy tended to walk or rent his transportation, but Patrick needed to ride.

That gave him a flash, a visual of Patrick above him, bouncing on his prick, sweat sheening the golden body.

"What are you thinking on so hard?" Patrick asked again, and Remy patted Patrick's round, firm buttocks.

"You'll see in time, *lapin*. Are you hungry?"

"I could eat three buffalo and wash them down with prairie dog stew."

"I would say that sounds foul but, sadly, I had both on the trail more than once. With tinned vegetables." He rolled off the bed so he could ring for an attendant.

Patrick covered himself with a sheet and watched him, blond head propped on his bent arm. "Have you travelled much?"

He'd told Patrick some of his sordid tale, but he would imagine the lad remembered very few of those early conversations. "From New Orleans to the far coast. San Francisco. On the way there I left early, so I took the northern trails. Faster. On the way back, I had to swing south. I've seen my share."

"Yes. The ocean. You've seen the ocean."

"I've seen both. There's one here, Patrick, and, when you're well, we'll cast our eyes upon it."

"I never even got to see the gulf." Patrick smiled. "There's a gorge I crossed once. That was the biggest thing I ever did see."

"I grew up on the water. She's a fickle mistress, and a demanding one."

"I hear tell of storms that wipe out everything in their path.

Walls of water and wind."

"You have tornados, though, *oui*? The great mother, she can punish us in so many ways. I saw an avalanche once. I never felt so scared of anything."

"We do. The worst is drought, though. That can scar a person to the bone."

"The land, too." Remy had a hard time imagining that. The swamps, they never dried. California always seemed foggy. The land in the middle, well, he'd passed through it like a haint.

"Yes. My people run a cotton mill. When the rains don't come, the world starts to starve." Patrick shuddered, as did the painting on the wall, and shook his head. "Henry was intended to run the mill, to marry a rich woman and make my father proud."

"Well, good thing you're not Henry." Remy understood disappointing a parent, but an illegitimate child had a much better chance of striking out on his own.

Patrick shook his head. "It would have been better that I lost my life than him, or so the story goes."

"I doubt that." A soft knock came at the door, and Remy opened it. "Ah. We're starving. What is the menu tonight, David?"

"Roast with potatoes, sir. The Master Colonel asked for something 'real and normal', sir."

"Did he, now?" Remy snorted. "We'll have two servings, then, and whatever they have for dessert."

Paddy was chuckling, the sound merry and bubbling from him.

"What, *bébé*? We might as well live high on the hog, *non*?"

"Yes, sir. I was thinking about the Colonel, about how, hearing that, I ain't surprised to have been sent here."

"No? He's a fascinating man, Matthias. So is Julian. I admit, I know little about our other owner. Of the club, I mean."

"There are three? Are they family somehow?"

Remy shook his head. "I have no idea, *cher*. There are rumors they're cousins. All related to the old man who began this place. For certain, they inherited when he died."

"Ah. Above me. I don't have a head for business or a care for it."

"I do all right." He preferred to win his money, but he managed the gold he'd won in California rather well.

Patrick shrugged and smiled, the expression bittersweet. "I was made for a different time, perhaps, when a man made his own way in the frontier."

"Mmm." Remy rather thought Patrick would make a fine kept man. He returned to the bed, needing more touch. Somehow he felt that Patrick had been held up to the looking glass of his twin and been found wanting, time and time again.

He had a feeling he would have preferred Patrick no matter what. Even if Henry had been a good man, there was something in Patrick that matched with him.

Something Remy had no intention of letting go.

Paddy reached out, traced the line of his collarbone, the caress openly and freely offered.

Remy closed his eyes and luxuriated in it a bit, the tingles of tiny lightning bolts buzzing under his skin. Patrick really had something deep inside him, an untapped power that thrummed with life.

He stroked the heavy mass of blond hair from Patrick's forehead, letting the raw silk strands fall through his fingertips.

Patrick arched like a cat, the contact making him hum and preen a little. So sensual. Untapped desire was Remy's favorite kind. He cupped Patrick's head, tilting it for a kiss, his fingertips finding a divot, a place under the scalp where the bone was dented.

Stilling, Patrick seemed barely to breathe. Remy moved away

from the spot, not lingering. He would find out later.

Patrick blinked at him, swaying as if they'd been indulging in far more strenuous exercise than they had. "You felt it too."

"Felt what, *bébé?*" He asked it lightly, wanting a spontaneous answer.

"That. That place."

"I did." A bullet, he thought. A ball. Definitely an injury.

"My brother was killed."

"He was." That spot seemed to addle Patrick some and he felt the urge to explore it, to touch again. Wickedness.

Instead, he kissed Patrick again, tasting sweat and confusion.

He had time to discover each and every one of his Paddy's secrets.

Tonight he would settle for just one or two.

Chapter Eleven

Patrick smoothed his waistcoat and then checked himself in the looking glass. He looked as dapper and normal as any of them. Remy insisted he wished to dine together in the dining hall and was waiting for him.

He told himself that there was no reason to worry. His manners were as good as anyone's, his stories more interesting because precious few people here in Baltimore would have been out the frontier as he had.

He opened the door, and David, the attendant he knew best, waited for him, eyes on the opposite wall. "Are you ready, sir?"

"Am I? Did I get all my bits and bobs on correct?"

"I believe so, sir." David still didn't look. "I'm blind, sir."

"Well then, if anyone takes me to task, I'll tell them you dressed me." Damnation.

A smile flashed across David's face, which was all stern angles and dark brows. "Yes, sir. I'll own up to it, if asked. This way."

"Lead on."

He followed, finding his nerves jangling like a dinner bell in the cotton fields. It was one thing to have supper with Remy and one or two friends. This was a public place, and he hadn't done that since before…

His mind skittered away from that thought, and he had a sudden image of Remy's dark eyes, like nighttime in the swamps.

The ringing backed off to a buzz, a hum of a dozen bumblebees. He shook his head, and even they dissipated.

David paced down the hall, taking him to a set of stairs, then down to the next floor, turning to the right and leading him around a mezzanine. This was the biggest place he'd ever seen. Ever, and he'd been to Dallas.

They rounded a series of halls and corners and David stopped by a large set of double doors carved with grapes and Greek gods. "The member dining room."

"Thank you, sir. I appreciate your help."

"Call for me anytime, Mr. Daniels. I am happy to help." David left him, a smile on his angular face.

All righty then. He pushed the door open, searching for Remy's familiar face.

He had to say one thing for this club, whatever it was. The members were a good looking bunch. Remy stood, then waved at him, and relief flooded him.

He headed over, the sound of the chandeliers clinking and clanking making him glance up.

"Now, *bébé*," Remy said when he reached Remy's side. "Breathe. Look into me, *oui*?"

"Remy." He met that dark gaze, his soul easing.

"You look very handsome." Remy took one of Patrick's hands between both of his.

"Thank you." He blushed dark, and sat at the table with its lovely cobalt dishes.

"I will introduce you about later, if you like. Perhaps over brandy." Remy watched him like a hawk.

"Of course. There are quite a few folks here."

More than he'd expected.

"This is the member dining room. There are oysters tonight, as well as a filet of beef and sweetbreads on toast. It's a popular menu."

Oysters. He'd never had those, but the other was familiar and lord knew he'd eaten every bit of strangeness any fancy officers table had laid before him. Hell, his people ate testicles.

"There's a Charlotte Russe for dessert. I am waiting for that." Remy winked.

He smiled and nodded, hoping that was code for apple pie or somesuch.

"It's a sort of cake. I never heard of it until I came here. It's too hot for it in the bayou."

"Do you miss it? Your crescent city?"

"Sometimes, when the moon is just right and I can hear the songs coming up from the deep." Remy shrugged. "I have a place here."

"Ah." He had never felt that, not since he was a boy. He remembered riding out in the fields and hiding in the cottonwood trees, stealing away from the lessons and the figures and the trappings of polite society in a lawless land.

Mother had come from Kansas City, drawn by Father's bluster and promise of being the height of society in Hunt County. He'd given her what she'd asked for, and she'd given him two sons—one of which was dead and the other...sent away, he supposed.

In disgrace.

The plates rattled on their chargers, and Remy put a hand over his.

"Breathe, *bébé*. You can do this. Talk to me."

"I don't understand."

"I know." Remy's smile was warm. "Together we will discover it."

The plates stopped shaking. Patrick breathed deep, smelling fresh bread. Oh, what a lovely scent.

"Is there anything as amazing as that smell?" Remy asked.

He nodded. "You."

Remy blinked, then a wide grin spread on his face. "Thank you, *bébé*. I love your scent, as well. It calls to me."

He did feel brash and wonderful, a little wild.

A waiter brought bread in a basket, the little white towel around it embroidered with a black raven. Bread and butter might be better than anything else they served.

He touched the cloth, traced the embroidery.

"It's something, isn't it? I always imagine little old ladies in a high garret, going blind over their embroidery by lamplight." Julian, who he had met before, stopped by their table, smiling at Patrick.

"My mother does this, but not quite so fine."

"My sisters did it poorly," Julian said. "I'm so pleased to see you out and about."

"Thank you, sir. Remy thought we ought to let our faces show."

Julian squeezed Remy's shoulder. "He's usually spot on."

A flash of jealousy hit him and the water glass before Remy split, right down the middle.

Waiters jumped forward, cloths in hand, and Remy barked out a surprised noise, eyes flying up to meet his. That dark gaze caught him, and he ducked his head, knowing somehow he was at fault.

Julian's low chuckle raised the hair on the back of his neck. "Careful, lad, or Remy will be forced to punish you. I'll leave you to it."

"I didn't touch the crystal," he protested.

"I know, *bébé.*" Remy smiled, that razor sharp grin that reminded Patrick of a hunting animal. "Do not worry. Just us here, hmm? That's all there ever is."

"I feel like everyone knows something I don't." And he didn't like it.

"I'm sorry." Remy's smile faded. "It's too soon to talk about it, Paddy. It upsets you. Soon, I promise."

"Have I done something terrible?" The table began to tremble and he held it down.

"No." The word settled across his shoulders, helping comfort him. Grounding him. "Not at all. Something was done to you. An injury. I know you trust me, *lapin*. Just believe all will be known in time."

"Thank God." He did not wish to be an outlaw, not truly.

"You are safe here, and I as much yours as you are mine. Do you understand?" When Patrick nodded, Remy pushed the bread toward him. "Try it."

"Thank you." He tore off a piece and offered the first bit to Remy.

Remy took it, fingers caressing his. The warmth in that touch shocked him, made him jump.

"You are a bundle of energy. I should have beaten you and made you spend before supper."

"Remy!" Such shocking things fell from Remy's lips.

"What?" Butter wouldn't melt in Remy's mouth. "It's the truth. Your bottom begs for my strong hand."

"You cannot say such things!"

"Why not?" Remy glanced about them. "No one is paying us any attention. This club lends itself to being permissive, especially in the member areas."

"Men do not do such things with one another." Did they? Surely not.

"No?" Remy raised a single brow before inclining his head toward the back wall of the dining room, where two men sat at a small table, hands linked across the top of the tablecloth.

He glanced over, then looked back to Remy, wide-eyed.

"I know it seems strange, but this is a safe place." Remy kept saying it, and Patrick was beginning to believe it.

He grabbed a piece of crusty bread for himself, buttered it, and allowed himself the luxury of enjoying it. His shoulders actually felt tired from sitting up about his ears, and he was pleased when they relaxed.

"Better, hmm? It is magic, the way it melts in the mouth."

"So good." He tore off another piece, feeling happier with every bite. His nerves must have burned away at him, leaving him empty as a worm.

The oysters arrived, sitting on their shells, but there were things in there with them, sauce and little vegetables.

"Remy?" He had no idea how to begin.

"Just so." Remy picked up a shell and a tiny fork that had been provided them. "Make sure it's loose." Remy poked it with the fork. "Then you toss it down."

"Toss it…" Oh, good lord.

"It's better than you think." Remy encouraged him with a smile before demonstrating.

He lifted the oyster shell and loosened the mass. He could do this. He could.

Remy nodded across from him, and he slipped it into his mouth and tossed his head back. Brine. That was what he tasted.

Brine and spice.

He swallowed, surprised to feel a heat building in his belly.

"You see?" Remy chuckled. "Now you know why people eat these?"

"Do you feel it as well?"

"I do." Remy picked up another oyster.

How odd. Fascinating. And he wanted to try another.

"Join me, *bébé*," Remy ordered.

He nodded and took a shell, loosening the muscle in time with Remy. They tossed their treats back together, and he licked his lips, his body warming even more.

His cock began to firm up, his belly tightening with a soft arousal. Patrick glanced about to make sure no one had noticed, but he jumped when Remy's foot slid against his under the table. "Only me."

"Only you." Demanding man. Still, it seemed to make the

world an easier place.

"No one else cares what we do. Not here. This is a little bubble." Remy's eyes seemed to glow with black fire.

"A bubble." He could fall into those eyes for miles. They were like the chasm he'd seen in the Badlands, eternal, immense.

"Ours. All we have to do is remember that. It takes discipline, but I can teach you."

He nodded, totally unsure what he was agreeing to, but willing to accept it.

"Good. Let's have the last two oysters."

"They are different things. You wouldn't think that a person would look at them and think you could eat them."

"I imagine a man saw some ocean creature pop one open and eat it. I think that with snails."

He nodded and chuckled, grateful that all the foods had surely been discovered by now, as large as the world was.

They sucked down the last oyster, washing it down with coffee and wine, and he felt plumb drunk by the time the filet of beef arrived. Now, that was pretty.

The room seemed more dim now, the candlelight low and intimate. He felt great warmth in his limbs, but also a kind of lethargy.

He inhaled deeply, the world seeming to sparkle about him, soft and strange.

The beef tasted like heaven, buttery and perfect. The demi-glace made him lick his lips in search of more flavor. Every time he licked, Remy chuckled, the sound scraping on his insides.

"That makes me imagine you licking my cock, *bébé*. So striking."

"Remy..."

The low laughter made his eyes cross. "There is sex magick in this room, late in the evening. Sink into it."

"Sex magick?" He'd never heard of such a thing, but he

could feel it in his balls.

"Mmm. *Oui*. Breathe." Remy's eyes seemed to glow. "We belong here."

"We do? I know you do." Remy was magical, no doubt about it. And Patrick did want to be with Remy so badly. He could do this. He'd eaten oysters, hadn't he?

Remy chuckled. "You shine like I've never seen before, *bébé*. You glow."

He swallowed hard. "It has to be the food, Remy. I'm—I need."

"Of course you do. Can you smell it? The scent of desire like perfume?" Remy made his head spin.

"I can. I— It's not just us."

"No, *mon doux*. That's why this is a members' only place. Everyone is hungry for one another."

"I'm only hungry for you." The words burned coming out of his mouth.

"Good." Remy used a piece of bread to soak up sauce, then nibbled it gently.

"Hey! I mean it. You...You make me feel like sinning."

"You were made for sinning with me alone, Patrick. Never doubt that." Remy's foot touched his again, then slid up his leg.

His johnson ached, the shaft full and throbbing, that illicit touch nearly too much to bear. He panted some, trying to remember where he was and why he was there.

"Soon I will have you on your knees, right here at the table, your mouth on my cock. Soon I will be your reward for a meal well enjoyed."

"I—" He couldn't breathe, and his insides shook. So did the table.

"It's only the truth, *bébé*. Nothing to fear. Look around you. See what it looks like to reward a good boy."

He shook his head. Looking would alter things for an eternity.

He knew this. He believed it.

Remy stood, then walked over to him to put a hand on his cheek. "Would that be so bad? To know things you never knew?"

He leaned into the touch, his heart beating so hard that he feared his chest would explode. Remy bent to kiss him, right there in front of God and everyone. He tensed, preparing to run, but the way those lips pushed against him, smashing his lips against his teeth, kept him bolted to the floor.

No one had ever kissed him so, not even Remy. The dinner plate pressed against his hand, the rim cold, almost sharp. He opened up to Remy's demand, taking the kiss as it went on and on, Remy's tongue sliding into his mouth. He swore he forgot to breathe, forgot to do anything but take the pressure of that plundering tongue.

Remy touched him then, one hand on his fly, and he nearly jumped out of his skin. They were at the dinner table!

The dishes clattered, the sound covering his needy moan.

A sharp pain in his lower lip made the world stop for a moment. Remy bit him, drawing all his focus. He groaned, his little rush of shock seeming to make Remy's eyes go black for the barest second.

"I could take you right here, Paddy. Spread you on the table and love you. I will someday." The low growl echoed inside him, perfect, wanton, hungry.

He didn't know what to do, so he lifted his chin, letting Remy bite at him. Those strong teeth had to be leaving marks on his skin.

Patrick refused to see the men around them. Refused. But he couldn't deny the sounds—moans and murmurs, hungry cries.

He soaked them in and, when Remy opened his trousers and pulled out his cock, Patrick just gripped the edge of the table and rocked his hips.

"No one has ever needed as you do, *bébé*. You burn so bright I can't resist."

"Please." He had no idea what else was going on around him. His whole world was that lean brown hand stroking him.

"Yes, *bébé*. So good. I'm so proud."

"Proud." What an exquisite feeling. His belly drew in, his cock thrusting up.

"Mmhmm. I will show you off to the world. My own."

"Anything." He was making wild promises, but the very air was made of desire, thick and pressing against his flesh, as if it was holding him close, keeping him inside his skin.

Remy licked at his chin, hand working faster, harder.

The candles began to glow, so bright, the light dancing as he arched. He couldn't make his eyes see correctly, everything blurring together, but he felt every impression of Remy's fingers on his cock.

"Please," he whispered. "Please."

"Yes. I want your seed, your scent. You've lasted the longest, *mon doux*, but it's time now. I'm ready."

A twist of the wrist, a none too gentle smack to the tip of his cock and he was coming, seed spraying over Remy's demanding hand.

Remy rewarded him with a kiss that left him sagging against the table and chair, dishes clattering to the floor in the wake of his hand when it slipped. Remy chuckled softly, then helped him sit, boneless and dazed.

He saw Remy lick his hand clean in what was becoming the most devastating habit on earth, and he did glance around then, seeing a room full of debauched men appearing as frazzled as he was.

The candles were burned to their nubs, the long tapers disappeared. He blinked, because the waiters moved about the room, replacing candles without so much as a twitch of their facial muscles.

"Dessert now, hmm?"

He moaned softly in answer. His cock was still out, the scent of his come on the air, and if Remy really did ask him to get under the table and put his mouth on that long prick, he would. Right now.

Remy chuckled as if his thoughts were written in a book, out there for anyone to read. "Not now, *bébé*." Remy plucked a napkin from the table to cover his lap. "They have Charlotte Russe."

"It must be one hell of a cake."

"It can be. Anticipation is an ingredient in all the best desserts. I want us both to wait for the next course of magick between us." Remy sat, then reached for his wine.

Sometimes it felt like Remy spoke a language foreign to him. He might never understand it, but he loved the sound of it.

Patrick tucked himself back in, making himself decent.

Remy gave him a disappointed look, a tiny pout. Lord, Remy could make his face say anything. The sounds of water being poured and plates being removed started up again.

"Does this happen here every night, Remy?"

"Not every night, no." Remy's laughter made him smile in return, infectious and happy. "Some nights there's just dinner."

"This is a fascinating place." Stunning. Patrick had never even dreamed of such a hideaway.

"It is. I can't wait to show you more." The waiter delivered a perfect tiny cake to their table, covered in jam and surrounded by some kind of cookie. How odd.

He waited for Remy to cut into it, the man obviously eager for the sweet. Remy sliced the thing in half, revealing cream and cake, and the confection did look appealing.

"That's the fanciest thing I think I've ever seen."

"It's a delicate art. The chef here has a way." Remy handed him a plate, then grabbed a fork, looking positively lustful.

Patrick thought that they should serve that sweet here daily, just so he could watch Remy enjoy it. As much moaning and fork licking as there was going on, Patrick might have to learn to make the damned thing himself.

He didn't even bother to try it; he just pushed his share over. "You should have it."

"Feed me a bite?" Remy opened up, lips shining, eyes dancing.

He carefully chose a bite, then leaned forward, offering it to his lover.

Remy nipped the cream and jam off the fork before leaning his elbows on the table. "This is a far better way to eat it."

"Yes?" He chose another bite, feeling so daring. "Is it sweet?"

"It is. Almost cloying, but saved by the jam and the biscuits, which are not sweet at all." Remy scooped up a bit on one finger to hold out for Patrick, daring him to suck it off, he thought.

He refused to look around, to see if anyone was watching before he dared to take the bite, actually nipping the tip of Remy's finger.

A short gasp was his reward. "Now, Paddy, you'll get everyone all het up again."

"Will I?" Had it been him? Maybe it only took a tiny nudge to set them all on that path.

"We will," Remy amended, reaching up to hold his wrist, the touch warm.

The tiny stroking contact burned him to the ground. His whole body jerked back on high alert in seconds as if he hadn't just spent himself like an untried lad.

"I do adore your passion." Remy stared at him, into him. Remy saw him.

"Have another bite of your sweet."

Remy chuckled, opening up for Patrick to feed him another forkful. Beautiful man.

He was becoming more than a fool for that happy smile. His

whole self needed Remy close, needed the attention and desire Remy showed him.

"I know, *bébé*. It is good, this between us."

"It is." Something broke loose inside him, something polite society usually kept tethered. He inhaled deeply, the flowers on the table spinning in their vase. How pretty!

Had they all bloomed like that when they sat down?

Remy fed him one more bite of cake before devouring the rest, even scraping the plate with his finger. "Cake sends all my good manners packing, *non?*"

"I like to see you feed your hungers."

"Do you?" Remy held out a hand, which Patrick took in his own. "I still have one from earlier."

"Do you?" He twined their fingers together.

"I do. I ache for your mouth."

His whole body heated, his cock jerking once again his trousers.

"As it is your first time, I believe I'd like to experience it in our quarters."

Patrick nodded, willing and eager, even if he had no idea what to do. They received several knowing smiles when they left the dining room, but not one shamed him. They were all in his boat, so to speak.

Remy hurried him along, the warrens of corridors making him plumb dizzy. They always seemed different, but maybe blind David only knew the most direct route.

"Easy. I know the way. This place knows me."

"Do you live here all the time?" He wanted to know everything about Remy.

"*Mais non*. I have a house. I can't wait to show you, *bébé*, but we'll stay here a while yet."

Such complicated things his Remy said.

He took them as gospel, though, because he had no choice in the matter.

They reached their room, and somehow it was home for now. Patrick breathed easier when the door closed behind them. He turned eagerly to Remy, reaching out. He wanted to touch, wanted to learn what Remy could teach.

Remy drew him to the low divan and sat them down, drawing his hand to Remy's hardness.

Patrick rubbed it through the cloth, amazed at how different it was to touch someone else. When he did it to himself he was furtive, half-ashamed.

Perhaps it was less a sin, to touch Remy. The way he felt about it, Patrick knew it was damned near sacred.

Remy helped him undo the buttons hidden in the placket of the fly, helped him pull out the long prick. "Slide off on your knees on the floor, sweet."

His cheeks burned, but he moved with it, his belly taut with a sudden, harsh need. He felt like a supplicant, and he allowed Remy to tug him forward by his hair, the crown of the heavy prick against his lips. He opened instinctively, his tongue flicking out to taste the salt and musk at the skin he found there.

"Yes. Just that way. Lick all around, Paddy."

The soft command was husky, hoarse, Remy's voice sibilant in his ears.

The command was easy to follow, and he ran his tongue around the rim, pushing at the extra skin there.

"Just so. Taste me, *bébé*. Know me."

He closed his eyes and nodded slightly. He savored the salt and bitter flavor of the heated drops Remy gave him, then explored the texture down the shaft. The veins throbbed against his tongue, and he tested them, pressed against them.

"*Oui.*" A rain of Creole French rained down on him, the words making no sense but he knew them. He dared to cup the soft sac, stroke it with his fingertips.

He felt Remy shake, the thigh muscles on either side of him

pulling tight. "*Bébé*, more. Give me more."

He didn't know what more meant here, but he took Remy as deeply into his mouth as he could.

He began to suck, pulling rhythmically, strong and steady. The move was surprisingly easy, and he bobbed his head, keeping his teeth away from the tender skin.

"Good. Good, just so. Just so, *bébé*. Taste me."

He was on the right track. Remy was petting him, stroking his hair, those strong fingers acting as something of a guide for him.

He ought to be ashamed, to do such a thing, to want such a thing, but he wasn't. He was hungry, eager. Remy tasted like everything good in the world, and the way that body curled around him made him work even harder. Remy's hand curled around his hand, petting him, encouraging him to move faster.

Patrick moved faster, if not deeper. Remy didn't push that, didn't ask him to do anything he couldn't.

His world began to spin, his soul caught in the center of Remy. All he knew was the hot flesh in his mouth, the sound of Remy's low, commanding voice.

"Only me." Remy repeated, again and again. "Only me."

Only Remy. Yes. He sucked, some instinct making him take a deep breath through his nose and go down as far as he could. He worked his throat muscles, trying not to choke.

"*Oui!*" Salty heat sprayed into his throat and he swallowed convulsively, taking the essence of Remy in. There was something so amazing about taking part of Remy inside him, and he couldn't imagine anything better.

The soft touches gentled and he found himself resting hard against Remy's thigh.

Remy raised his face up to take a kiss. "Thank you, *lapin*. You honor me."

"Never had a supper like this before."

"I hope it won't be our last." Remy grinned that razor sharp smile. "I rather love that we pushed our peers a bit tonight."

He wasn't sure what that meant, but he reached up to stroke Remy's smile.

He had a feeling he had a lot more to learn, but he knew by now that Remy would teach him anything he wanted to know.

Chapter Twelve

You and your boy put on quite a show last night, Remy." Remy glanced up from the breakfast array, which was laid out in chafing dishes on a pair of enormous trestle tables. He understood from David and Anek that many members had spent the night last night after supper became so heated.

He smiled at Canaan, who he'd expected to be on his way back to Texas by now. "He's something else, no?"

"He is. Are you going to give him back to his family?" Wicked man.

"No." Remy selected some bacon and a pile of eggs, knowing Patrick would need his strength. "Is that why you're still here, *cher*? To wait and see?"

"Idle curiosity. He created mass chaos. I wonder at his depths."

"Oh, *cher*. He's *fort, oui*? Strong. He's learning so fast, too." He paused, trying to pick a few sweets. "Do you know how he was injured?"

"He took a ball to the back of his head. He was dragging his dead twin off the field, or so his father says."

"Oh, *chou*. That explains the divot." Remy shook his head, his heart aching for his sweet Paddy. "I think he didn't do what he does until he got hurt."

"That doesn't surprise me. His people would have drowned him at birth if he'd done all that mess early on."

"Or burned him at the stake, hmm?" He chose a roll with

candied apricots and one with nuts and spices.

"You haven't met the senior Daniels. I wouldn't put it past the man."

Remy scowled at Canaan. "Well, he never needs to go back there."

"He's been promised to his brother's woman, you know?"

"So you said before." Remy would not give Patrick back to those people. No. Patrick was his now, would be dead without him. A life debt, some indigenous people called it. Patrick's soul belonged with his, no question.

Canaan laughed. "Good luck, my friend. Any time you need help with lessons…"

A flash of possessive passion hit him in a rush, like a wave of heat. "The best I can promise is when I need someone to watch," Remy said lightly.

"He's not hard on the eyes. I could admire."

"If I bound your hands that's all you could do." He selected one more delicate pastry, this one with lemon curd for Patrick. "Breakfast. I'll see you later, *mon ami*."

"Have a lovely day, you tease." Canaan was altogether too pleased with himself.

Remy shook his head, wanting to hurry back to Patrick. He needed to see his lover all of a sudden. Feed him.

Build a new hunger inside Patrick's soul.

That was something far more precious to Remy than anything ever had been.

Chapter Thirteen

Patrick went searching for food. He had spent three days talking and touching, tasting and laughing with Remy, the time flying by as they did little but learn one another. It was an addiction.

Remy was so kind, so good about going to the breakfast room and picking out the perfect morsels. Patrick wanted to return the favor.

He'd been out three times, but the way seemed...odd. Confusing. Wrong.

He'd been paying attention the last time, really watching the turns, but...This was wrong.

Patrick paused, looking about and wishing he had rung for David. He just hadn't wanted to wake Remy. When he turned, he found himself facing a wall. No. No, wait. That wasn't right.

Stopping, hands clenched into fists, Patrick took a deep breath. "Now, don't get all het up," he murmured.

Obviously he'd done got himself all turned around, woolgathering so that he didn't know which end was up.

He decided to retrace his steps but, when he turned back, nothing appeared familiar.

A dull worry bloomed inside him, making him frown and reach back, scratch the ache inside his head. The portrait of some ole feller next to him rattled, then slid to the floor with a thunk.

Right. Right, count the paintings. Wig guy. Yellow feather hat. Duck hunter. Naked...Oh, dear lord. Patrick peered at the writing forms on the canvas. Could you even do that?

He blinked at the sight of a man's hand disappearing into… Dear.

His heart pounded just thinking of it. With Remy… Oh, God.

No. No, it couldn't be possible. That was a flight of fancy, one of a very perverted mind.

He turned away, then looked back, blinking as the painting that appeared was one of a muscled man bound in leather on a velvet coverlet.

Wait. Wait, he had only…

He began to shudder, a cold sweat pouring over his body and the paintings began to clatter on the walls. All of them.

Patrick staggered, then righted himself. He lumbered down the hall, searching for his door.

He didn't need food. He needed Remy. He bounced against a door, gasping in shock as it popped open, exposing three men writhing naked on the bed.

"Sorry. So sorry." He ran, careening around a corner, his panic rising.

The floor trembled beneath his feet, hard enough to knock him to his knees. Patrick clapped his hands over his ears when the lamps overhead began to jangle, their globes swaying. "No! No, stop! Remy! Remy, can you find me?"

He groaned, imagining those dark, dark eyes. *Remy, please.*

Paddy? Oh, God, he could hear Remy calling to him. He rocked back and forth, trying to be a beacon in this dark place.

The walls are moving.

Breathe. Think of me. My touch. Only me. I'm coming.

"Only you."

Only his angel. He repeated it over and over, his hair feeling as if it was trying to crawl off his head.

Then Remy's hands came down on his shoulders, that lean

body pressing against his back. "There you are, *bébé*."

"The walls moved, Remy. The walls moved."

"Shh. We need to talk but not now. Come, *bébé*. Back to our room."

"How?" He sobbed softly, his head throbbing, his world spinning. "Do you know the way?"

"I do." Remy tugged him to his feet before turning him about, those almost black eyes boring into his. "Me. Look at me."

"Remy. The walls moved." Walls couldn't move.

"Shhh."

A door opened, and an Injun man stepped out, long hair falling down over his chest. "Remy? Do you need help?"

His eyes went wide and he simply stopped breathing for a second. "Don't you hurt him. I won't let you."

"No, Koni. We're fine. Fine. Tell the Colonel I am aware he wants to speak to me."

The man nodded and disappeared back into the door he'd come through.

Remy took his hand. "Please, Paddy. We must move."

"I'm sorry. Forgive me." Remy would send him away. He'd done it again, he'd caused things to be...wrong.

"Never. You're mine." The fierce words got his feet moving again.

"Yours." Wouldn't that be something, for that to be right?

"Yes." Remy dragged him down three long halls, surely much farther than he'd ever walked.

The door to their room was open, and he panted, speeding his steps to get inside.

"Remy." He stumbled into the room, almost going to his knees.

Remy closed the door behind them. "What were you about, *bébé*? You're not ready to take on the club alone."

"I wanted to bring you food. You have been so good to me."

"Oh, *lapin*, that's dear of you." Remy sank to the rug with him, kissing him, holding his cheeks with both hands.

"The walls moved, Remy, and the pictures...they changed."

"This is a magical place, *bébé*." Remy kissed him between words. "Powerful. You're vulnerable to it now, but soon you won't be."

"I don't understand." He clung to Remy like a limpet, swaying against the man like he was buffeted by waves.

"I know. I do." Remy kissed him harder, hands working at his blouse and trousers.

He opened to the pressure of those hard lips, gasping as he let himself sink deeper and deeper into the pleasure. That was the way, wasn't it? The way to escape the madness trying to overtake him. Patrick let Remy transport him, surround him, protect him. He needed this, needed someone to help him.

"I have you." Remy pushed him down on his back. Those clever hands stripped him of his clothing, leaving him bare as a babe, but he had no time for embarrassment. Remy scratched his chest, pinching his nipples one after the other.

The sting made his toes curl, made him twist and moan, his body responding like he was made for nothing else. He spread his legs when Remy pushed at his thighs, then pressed one knee down on the floor between them. When Remy leaned over him, that lean thigh slid against his cock. The pressure made him ache, and he found himself pressing back, taking more, asking for more.

Remy hummed, the sound easier now, not so worried. "*Oui. We're all the magick you need right now. You need this, this right here, sweet baby."

"Yes." Patrick nodded, those dark eyes staring into his, almost hypnotic.

"Yes." Remy pushed and eased back just before the ache became pain.

Patrick panted, his body shaking, his cock hard as it had ever been. When Remy slapped it with the flat of one hand he jerked, gasping, the pain intensifying the need riding him.

"You can't!" But Remy had.

In fact, Remy did it again, then tugged down on his balls, making his legs draw up.

He shuddered, the fire in the hearth popping and snapping, and Remy tugged again. "*Non, bébé*. Right here."

"I can't! I don't know what to do!"

Remy slid one hand lower, beneath his balls, a finger pushing right inside his body. "Yes, you do."

His eyes went wide and his body clamped down, the sudden invasion huge. Remy's touch scraped along his nerves, sending shudders up and down his spine and making him bare his teeth.

"This is the beginning, *bébé*. The start."

"The start of what?"

"The way for you to find your center. Your balance." Remy sounded like a damned mystic, like one of them medicine men.

"Just breathe." Remy pressed deeper, that one finger going deep.

He inhaled, filling his lungs with air that seemed to tingle. His vision swam with spots, and he arched, trying to make more room in his chest for air.

"Focus. Focus on me and me alone."

"I'm *trying!*"

"I know that, *bébé*. I do. But you must try harder. I need to give you more."

"More?" His mind didn't understand it a bit.

"So much more." Remy leaned across him, reaching with that free hand for something he couldn't see. "Do you trust in me? Believe in me?"

"You're my angel."

"Then open to me." Remy uncapped a vial of oil, tugged out

of Remy's valise which lay on the floor.

"Open to you." He felt drugged, as if the magicks themselves held him close.

"Yes, *lapin*. Let me in." Remy poured oil between his legs, trickling it where finger met hole.

The slick liquid changed from cool to hot with a shocking speed, making him gasp. In fact, it burned a tiny bit, making Patrick squirm.

"It has a bit of warming in it." Remy pushed two fingers inside him now.

"A bit."

Remy touched him deep, stroking him, and the touch liked to set him aflame. He'd never felt such a thing in all his life as Remy's fingers slipping in and out, the oil burning him but not scarring.

"Beautiful boy. I will have every inch of you. Every inch."

"I would give you everything."

"Believe me. You will." In and out, Remy stretched him, pushed him. His sac drew up and his prick left blistering drops on his belly. He tried to move, but Remy held him fast with one hand on his belly. "Take what I give you, *bébé*."

"I am." He shook his head, maddened by the pushing and stretching, his body lit up like a thousand fireflies inside him.

"There's more." Remy withdrew, then trickled more oil down on his hole.

"More?" His thighs spread, trying to make room inside him.

"Yes, Paddy. Hold your legs wide. I need space."

Remy spoke words that made no sense, but he obeyed regardless. When Remy muscled up between his thighs, he still didn't understand. Not until Remy pressed his cock to Patrick's entrance. Patrick gasped, the touch near blistering.

"Shh." Remy stroked his belly. "Take a deep breath, and then let it out."

Those eyes were jet, and he could see the universe in them as he sucked in a lungful. He let it out slowly, relaxing his body, and that was when Remy slipped inside him, all the way, hips meeting his ass.

"Remy." The word was the only thing in his soul, in his mind. The only thing.

"*Oui*. Oh, sweet *bébé*. So hot inside." Remy petted him, his belly and chest, before pinching his nipples hard. He gritted his teeth and arched, his body clenching. That made Remy cry out, the sound shocking and wild.

Remy began to move, pressing deep. Inside him. Remy and he were one. The tugs to his now-aching nipples continued and he found himself lost, spinning wildly in utter pleasure. The only thing pinning him down was his lover.

His lover.

His angel.

"Just so. As you are mine." Remy stared into him, hands slipping down to his hips, the grip bruising.

"Yours. Please." He didn't know what he begged for, but he knew it was the right thing to do.

Remy nodded, face set in hard lines, and rocked harder into him, moving fast enough that their skin slapped together.

He began to meet each thrust, adding his strength to Remy's, their bodies trying to meld into one. He could only reach Remy's thighs, the very lowest part of his belly, but Patrick wanted to feel Remy move.

"Mine. Mine. Mine." The words pinned him down, kept him where he was.

Patrick nodded frantically, his body on fire, moving in time with every thrust Remy pounded into him. His body felt cracked open, spread wide. He couldn't breathe, could only see Remy. The place where they joined heated every second, the spiced oil making Patrick cry out.

Remy nodded, sweat sheening the lean, angular face, and he reached up, cupped Remy's cheek as Remy bent down to kiss him. His cock rubbed Remy's belly, finally receiving friction, and he cried out, near desperate for it.

The kiss stole what was left of his breath, Remy sending him right out of his mind. When Remy's hand closed around his cock, he shot, seed spraying from him. He lost all control, ceded it all to Remy. Every bit.

From a distance, he felt the heat of Remy, filling him, marking him inside. Remy shouted his name, the syllables completely unfamiliar in the lilting accent.

He melted, sinking into the rug. His hands fell to his sides, his chest heaving while he fought for breath.

Remy slumped against his chest, one hand over his thundering heart. "Don't leave without me again, *mon doux*. Not for a bit, yet."

"Forgive me. I was trying to do good by you."

"You did." Remy pressed a kiss to his chest. "I am very proud, *bébé*. Very. Never doubt it."

"Will they send me away?" he asked, terrified for the answer but refusing to not ask the question.

"No." Remy said it so firmly he had to believe. "No, I will make sure not."

"Thank you. I didn't mean to get lost."

"I know that. This place." Remy rose up, smiling faintly into his eyes. "It can confuse a man."

"Yes. I swear to you, the walls moved."

"Mmm." Remy slipped free, leaving him feeling grasping and empty. "Come to bed. We'll ring for breakfast today."

He nodded, his entire body shuddering, his world upended. Patrick crawled into bed with Remy, clinging to the one thing in the universe that seemed real.

"Shh. Shh, *bébé*. All is well. I have you, you have my word."

"I believe you." He would believe because Remy told him to. And because Remy was becoming everything to him.

Remy was becoming the entire world.

Chapter Fourteen

Remy left Patrick sleeping deeply, the draught Anek had slipped him to that purpose working perfectly. Not poppies, because he didn't want to fight the demons with Patrick again. Just something to make him rest well.

Remy felt like a disappointing child being called to carpet when he entered the meeting room. The Colonel was there, along with Julian, Koni and Giles, the archivist.

He let none of that show, nodding easily at them all. "Is there coffee?"

"Of course there is." Giles' voice was like silk. "Daniel."

Daniel moved about, pouring cups of coffee and laying out plates of petits fours. So civilized.

Remy nipped a bite of one; lemon and blueberry. Lovely.

"He's a danger, son." That was the Colonel, practical and brutally straightforward. "He damn near opened us up, straight through the center."

"He didn't, though. You must admit, the first encounter alone with the Raven is unnerving."

"Why was he alone, dear one?" Jules asked. "When you know how uncontrolled he is."

"I was asleep." Remy shrugged, trying to stay elaborately casual. "He wanted to bring me breakfast."

"Oh. That's so sweet…" Giles was the eternal romantic.

"Isn't it?" He smiled at Giles, whose little spectacles glinted in the light. "I vow, he knows better now."

"Mayhap you ought to tie him to the bed, then, when you sleep."

"Perhaps we might have to prevent him from calling things here that we are not yet prepared to fight." The Colonel's voice was soft, deadly.

Koni put a hand on the Colonel's shoulder. "He is powerful, friend Remy. Too powerful."

"He's learning. He is learning to control himself. I swear to you." Remy held out his hands, supplicating. "I know now that I cannot be slow. I will speed his training."

"His gifts are vast, Blanchard. The demons will hear him and they will come."

"Not if he learns, and he will. He was frightened. He's not even aware that he is doing it!"

"That makes it worse." The Colonel sighed. "Better to cut it off now."

"No! I will take him back to New Orleans if I must. Leave you out of it. But I will not let you kill him."

"Nonsense." Everyone looked at Giles, who blinked rapidly. "We depend upon Remy for certain matters, Colonel. We cannot lose him."

"We cannot risk notice."

"We risk notice every day," he argued.

Julian nodded. "We do, but your boy is rather a spectacular beacon."

"Let me have a fortnight. I will teach him what he needs to know."

Julian looked at Giles. "Will the wards hold?"

"They will, but not against many blows like this morning. He's incredibly powerful. Raw."

"I'll help reinforce them," Remy murmured.

"If you can't control him, he won't suffer." The Colonel's words were cold as ice.

Remy shook his head. "No. No, he will learn in time."

He believed that. Paddy would learn and then Remy would

bring him to his home on the harbor.

"We'll give you another chance, then," Julian said. "But be aware. We only have so much leeway."

"He can learn." Patrick's soul was pure, decent. His *bébé* wanted to control himself.

"Then prove it." The Colonel stood, holding out a hand to Koni, who took it and nodded. "You have a fortnight."

"A fortnight." He would take the time and run with it.

"Yes. We revisit this then."

"Yes. Of course. We will make it work for us."

"Thank you, *ami*," Julian said. "I'll check in with you."

Remy nodded, and they left him there with Giles, who cleared his throat.

"What is your plan, exactly?" Giles asked.

Remy smiled at him, then lifted his cup. "I have no idea, exactly."

"Perhaps I could be of assistance, then? I record all of the inhabitants here, their activities."

He glanced sideways at Giles, then nodded slowly. "I have been… training with him. Making him focus on me. Absorbing his energy."

"Good. Good. You should perhaps bind him at night until he has found his control."

"Oh." Remy warmed to that thought, his Paddy, stretched out and tied, all of his will taken. "I can do that."

"I can provide you with implements of wickedness, sir. Wooden phalli, leather floggers and bindings, unguents and oils that sting and heat."

He blinked at Giles, more than a little shocked. One wouldn't think Giles would be so well-versed.

The bright eyes twinkled from behind Giles' glasses, the expression suddenly wicked. "I am no virgin, you know."

"*Non, ami*. You are a member here." That spoke to perversion in the best way.

"I most certainly am. Come, friend. Let us explore the storerooms. After all, we must protect our members to the fullest extent, yes?"

How had Remy not seen this delicious evil shining from Giles ere now? His alligator spirit felt kinship here.

"That we do, *mon ami*. That we do." They smiled at each other, and Remy felt a sharp sting of excitement.

He had a feeling Giles was about to show him things even he had never thought of.

Chapter Fifteen

atrick woke up slowly, his head ringing with the oddest emptiness, as if the world was a cracked bell that was being tapped, so gently.

He looked around for Remy, but found himself alone. He forced down his immediate panic. Remy would return. He always did. Besides that, he was no child. He had been a soldier, faced down Comanche. He would not be afraid.

He stood, hunting the wash basin. Patrick felt sticky, gritty. It was like he'd been in a battle, and he knew better. He knew he'd been here. Perhaps he'd been battling his own madness.

The door opened with a soft click of the latch. Remy entered, hauling a heavy leather bag. That smile sent shivers right down his spine.

"Did you rob a bank, Angel?" he teased, covering himself with a towel.

"No. I did raid the archives. Fascinating place." Remy strode over and took away the cloth.

"The archives? Books?" He blinked at Remy. "I was washing up."

"Not exactly, though I did find one tome Giles assures me I may read so long as I remain in the library." Remy kissed him, a short, hard peck of lips. "Shall we have a bath?"

"Please." He did enjoy the feel of water around him, buoying him up. "I'm sorry I slept so long."

"You had a bad time of it." Remy patted his privates, which made him jump. Familiar man.

Yes, well, the walls had moved.

Remy laughed, the bag sitting by the door, forgotten, Patrick thought. Remy loved a bath. It was good, to have Remy laughing, to know that, whatever business his lover had been out on, it hadn't been distasteful.

The bath ran, Remy touching him in a dozen tiny ways, a hand on his hip, fingers rubbing his ass.

His cock responded, filling eagerly. He flushed, his belly and balls pulled tight. The things Remy did to him.

"In the tub, *bébé*."

"Will you come in?" he dared to ask.

"I will. Nothing would please me more. Let me get us a few things."

Patrick nodded and slipped into the warmth, the silky water. He let his head loll back against the edge, his toes gripping the bottom of the tub.

It soothed him, down to the ground.

Remy slipped in moments later, sleek as one of those otters he'd read about.

"Good morning, Remy," he murmured.

"Good morning, *lapin*. You slept hard."

"Like a log. I feel good now, rested."

"You look it. Which is good, *bébé*. I have big plans."

"Yes?"

"Oh, *oui*. Vast."

Vast. He chuckled softly, daring to touch Remy's hip, trace a line down the smooth skin.

"Mmm. Yes, *mon doux*. Touch me."

"My pleasure." He wanted to explore, so he soaped up a cloth, taken from the rack by the tub, feeling about as brave as he ever had. It fascinated him, though, the way the suds bubbled over Remy's skin. He loved the contrast of the soap and Remy's dusky flesh, loved how slick everything got.

He leaned close, drawing a lazy circle on Remy's ribs.

"Tickles!" Remy snapped at him playfully, white teeth close to his skin.

"Sorry." He lied.

"I think not." Remy dug into his ribs with one hand.

Patrick hooted, splashing as he wriggled. "Remy! Tickles!"

"See? You did it apurpose."

"Not. I swear to you, I did not!"

Remy laughed hard, head thrown back, so beautiful it hurt to look at him. He didn't look away, though, not for a second. He loved that look, craved it. Oh, he needed all of Remy's expressions.

He stole a kiss, soft and careful against Remy's throat.

Remy petted his hair. "You're good to me."

"Am I?" He worried that he wasn't.

"You are. No one ever had such a care." Remy could be so closed... So contained. He didn't look that way now.

"I'm sorry for that, but I'm pleased I can be. Caring. Yours. Right."

"You're perfect, *bébé.*" Remy lay full out atop him, the water lapping around them.

He held on, hands moving constantly, dragging and stroking and petting. Remy gave as good as he got, hands busy on his skin. Then Remy reached over the side of the tub to pull up something he'd left on the floor. Patrick's hand slipped down and wrapped around Remy's ass, holding on for a brief second.

"I told you I brought you some things, *mon doux,*" Remy said.

"Mmhmm?" He focused on the sweet throat, on Remy's jaw.

"I think you'll like this." Remy lifted his chin to kiss him.

He pushed into the kiss, a slow burn sparking in the pit of his belly. He licked and lapped at Remy's mouth because he knew now where these drugging kisses led. He was fast becoming an addict.

When Remy held something up for him to see, though, Patrick paused. It was a small leather sleeve with laces along one side.

He frowned, confused, trying to work out what it would sheathe.

Remy smiled, the toothy grin that always meant he was about to start something shocking. He reached up, traced the shape of Remy's lips, curious but cautious.

"You ready, *bébé*?" Remy stroked the leather over his throat.

"I reckon, for not knowing what you're up to."

"This is a binding ring. It will go here." Remy reached down into the water to close one hand around the base of Patrick's cock.

His eyes went wide, pulling at the corners as his hips surged up toward Remy's fingers.

"*Oui.* You see. I will put it on you, and it will keep you hard during all the games I wish to play."

"I—" His eyes went wide and his thighs clenched, shook the barest bit.

Remy's dark, direct gaze bored into him. "You trust me, *cher.* I know it."

"Yes. Yes, I do." Beyond all reason.

"Then kneel up and let me put it on you." That happy laugh would have made Patrick do anything.

"You're on top of me, Remy."

"Oh." Remy nipped his throat. "So I am. It's good it's a big tub."

"I've never seen the like. Does every room have one?"

"Not all of them. One has a rainbath, you know? Where you can stand and get clean."

"A rainbath?" Fascinating. He thought he'd prefer the tub, still.

"Mmm. We'll have to borrow it sometime soon. There will

be times when you have to stand to bathe." Remy laughed, the sound making his balls ache.

He wasn't sure why he'd ever need to stand and bathe, not with this tub, but he didn't answer or question. Remy would only explain, and much more debauchery and he'd spill.

"Up now, *bébé*, and offer me your cock."

Remy slid off his lap and helped him kneel up. Patrick stared while Remy wrapped the leather around the base of his cock and began to lace it. The pressure wasn't bad, more a caress, a steady, easy circle around his shaft.

The tiny bit of extra sensation made Patrick catch his breath.

"Very nice. Now, come and sit."

"But Remy, the leather…" It would tighten, if it got wet.

"Yes?" Remy touched it, rubbing the leather against his skin.

"It can't get wet. It will ruin."

"No, *lapin*. It will shape to you. I swear, you will not ruin it." Remy licked his lips, staring down at Patrick's hardness. His body seemed to thrum, shaft bobbing as he lowered himself into the water.

He panted when Remy kissed him, the fire burning under the surface flaring to life, passion burning him. The hand on his cock moved, stroking him, flicking the tender slit with each upstroke.

The tip of his prick became so sensitive he had to grab Remy's hand, stopping the movement.

"Oh now. Don't spoil my fun, *bébé*."

"Tender," he protested.

"I know." Remy pinched his slit shut. "It's mine to play with as I will. This is what you must learn."

His thighs tightened and he gasped, the water slapping against the walls of the tub.

"So obedient." Remy moved those tormenting fingers, teasing him. One finger pressed against his tip, rubbing hard and he sat up, the world shuddering for a long moment.

Then Patrick took a deep breath, focusing on Remy. Watching, waiting for his next cue.

"*Oui.* Just so, *bébé.* You can learn this."

"I don't understand."

Remy slid closer, slipping up to rest against his side. "You keep saying that, but I believe you know in your bones what I want."

"I do not…" He groaned softly, reaching for Remy's hip.

"*Non.*" Remy stopped his action with the single word. "Not this time, *mon doux.* I touch you. Hands behind your neck, if you please."

He felt another shudder ripple through the air. "Behind…"

No. No, he couldn't, but he did, didn't he? Patrick raised his hands to place them behind his neck, leaving the whole of his body exposed.

"Good. Good, just so." Remy met his gaze, so steady. "You focus on me and me alone. I will be your center."

"Please. I'm so confused."

"I'm here with you. I will never let you fall, Patrick." The lilt deepened in Remy's voice, the promise ringing in his ears. Echoing.

Focus. Focus. The words spun inside him.

"Perfect boy." Remy slapped his prick through the water, the sound far more shocking than the feeling.

"What do you want from me?" He didn't understand—not any of this, least of all his reaction.

"I want you to be with me, Paddy. To experience all I can teach you. Obedience comes naturally to you, and it's what you need so badly."

Could that be so? He had run from his father, from the mill. He went to do his duty in the service to protect Henry, to see more than the cotton fields of his home.

Hell, his sainted mother had said he was the most disobedient child she'd ever seen. How could Remy see compliance in him? Engender it, even.

The spot in the back of his head began to throb, the water spinning.

"No, sweet. No thinking too hard." Remy slapped his cock again; this time the leather held it stiffer.

"Remy!" His fingers clenched into fists as he arched.

"Look at you. Beautiful. So much pleasure awaits."

He spread his legs, trying to make room for the sensations within him. His balls swung, feeling separated from his cock, his belly tight and hard.

Remy moved his leg, draping first one over the edge of the tub, then the other.

"What are you doing?" He had to ask, even if he wasn't sure he wanted to know.

"Spreading you wide, *bébé*. Opening you right up."

"I can't balance."

"Then put your hands down to grip the sides of the tub. I'm glad you tell me what you need."

His belly tightened, his abs rippling as he reached down and grabbed the tub. Patrick felt exposed, even with the water covering some of his lower body.

Remy touched him, palm sliding under his balls to lift them, roll them and push them against his body.

A sound escaped him, a cross between a whimper and a grunt. He pushed up, trying to get away.

"*Non*. No, *bébé*. Right there, if you please."

"I can't—"

Remy pushed harder, face set in stern lines. "You can and you will. Stay where you are."

The snap in Remy's voice shocked him, made him still.

Remy pressed and rolled his balls in their sac, then pressed two fingers from the other hand against his hole. His body clenched of its own accord, and he squeezed his eyes shut.

"Shh. Remember how we do this, Paddy. Breathe in, then out. Push with your hips."

He did remember or, if he didn't, his body did. Patrick sucked in a gust of air, then let it out, his ass relaxing, the touches addicting as the taste of rum.

Moreso, maybe. He'd never been one for strong drink.

This was more than he could resist, more than he wanted to resist. He panted, his muscles rippling, his body fighting to accept the invasion. Remy gave him no quarter, pushing in and in, spreading him wide. His cock felt too tight, too hard, his balls heavy and throbbing.

The water moved with his body, but nothing else swirled or shook. There was only Remy.

"See? You have this. You can do this."

He wasn't sure what Remy spoke about, but he found he didn't care. All that mattered was callused fingers and wet leather and the sounds Remy made. Sharp teeth found his nipple, the sting enough to make him gasp.

Patrick shook, but he held himself still, the tub creaking under his grip.

Remy licked his other nipple, then blew a stream of air over it and the sudden cold made his nipple draw up tight and hard.

His cock jerked in its binding. "Please, Remy."

"All in good time, *bébé*. All in good time."

"No. I can't bear it." He shook his head, feeling frantic. The room seemed to shake, to shiver much like his soul was doing now.

"You can. You're strong. *Fort.*" Remy's tone brooked no argument.

He gasped air in, the room seeming to spin, the chandelier tinkling in time with his heartbeat.

Remy pinched his bound cock, gathering the tiny bit of loose skin at the head. "Paddy!"

"What? What!" He blinked, meeting Remy's gaze again.

"Pay attention." Remy held his gaze, held his cock, the pressure insistent.

He bared his teeth, fighting against the tremors that moved... in him? Outside of him? He didn't know. "I don't understand what's happening!"

"What's happening is I'm making love to you. I need you here with me, not worried about what anyone else might think."

"I'm not. I don't know how to feel all this!"

"But you don't have to." Remy took his face between both palms, staring into his eyes. "I know. You follow my lead."

"The world wants to move, to shake apart." He let go of the tub with one hand, touching that awful divot in his skull.

"No." Remy grabbed his wrist. "No, it's not the world, *bébé*. You know that."

"It's big." Too big. Not Remy, the world.

"It is big. We can handle it together." Remy kissed him again, one hand cradling the back of his head so gently.

Remy stroked that spot, and his eyes rolled with the lightning that buzzed through him.

"Shh. My brave soldier." Remy kissed his lips over and over. "You have to see, Paddy. You have to understand before we can make it better."

"I didn't mean to," he moaned. "I swear to you. I meant no harm."

"Never. You are honorable." Remy crawled into his lap, rubbing their cocks together.

"Yes. Yes, I am a good man."

"My good man."

"Yours." He swallowed hard. If he belonged to Remy it was up to Remy to decide what to do, right? "Can we make it go away? Can we kill it?"

It must be a devil, crouching inside him.

"Oh, *bébé*. It's not the enemy. You'll see once we control it. It's a gift, but it takes time." Remy was smiling now, rubbing their noses together.

He didn't understand. He simply couldn't. "Please help me."

"I am. I will." Those beautiful eyes flashed gold and, for a moment, he thought Remy might simply tear his throat out. Then they were kissing, the heat between them such he thought they would ignite.

Remy began to touch him again, nails dragging on his wet skin, teasing him. Goosebumps rose on his skin, and he gasped, his legs straining under the pressure of Remy's weight. He let all his aches, all his need push into Remy, spread through them both.

Remy hummed, the sound thrumming through him, so that must be right. They rocked together, Remy scraping at him with close-clipped nails.

"Remy. Please."

"Tell me what you want, *bébé*." Remy stared at him, and he felt as though this was some sort of test.

"I want you to...I want to feel you again, filling me. It's the only time I feel quiet inside."

"Anything, *mon doux*. I would give you anything." Remy slid back between his legs, kneeling on the bottom of the tub.

"I need you," he whispered. "I need your touch."

"You have it." Remy reached over the side of the tub again, but it was oil he brought up this time. "I want you, too. Together, *bébé*, we will discover the world."

"Promise?" He panted, his legs moving, his ass sliding against the porcelain. He was ready.

"Yes, Paddy. I swear." Remy's fingers pressed inside him, the stretch immediate and fierce, wild.

"I want to see. To be with you." He opened up, bore down,

all the things Remy had taught him.

Remy groaned for him, fingers driving into him again and again, offering him no quarter, demanding that he live this pleasure. He couldn't escape, so Patrick gave into it, using his grip on the tub to shove his hips toward Remy.

"Greedy lover." Remy's words were dark, harsh on the air.

"I'm sorry."

Remy pushed inside him, those fingers curling to find a spot that made him shout. "No. No apologies. Never apologize for needing me."

"Yes." Something was missing there. Something… "Yes, sir."

"Oh." Remy looked at him as if he hung the moon. "Yes, *bébé*. Just so."

Remy stroked that spot within him, over and over until his heart climbed into his throat, almost choking him. Patrick wailed, his cock jerking but not letting loose. His balls drew up so tight, but nothing happened.

Remy's smile was all teeth and Patrick knew Remy saw everything.

Those fingers finally slid free, but the pressure only increased when Remy pushed in with his cock, the burn immense.

"Do not let go, *bébé*. I decide how fast we go, how far. Just me."

"Only you," Patrick agreed. They were the only things moving in the room. The only thing moving inside him was Remy.

Patrick squeezed down, wanting Remy to feel as good as he did, wanting him desperate. Remy gritted his teeth, sensation seeming to flare between them.

Moving faster, Remy slammed into him, hand on his cock. Those fingers worked him unmercifully and he found himself whimpering, begging for his lover, for his completion.

"Not yet." Remy pushed him higher and higher every second. "I want to watch you, Paddy. See you come apart for me."

He didn't understand. Surely Remy could see him. Still, whatever his lover offered, he would take. He threw his head back, arching up to get more of that fine cock inside him.

"Such need. So eager to learn." Remy slammed into him. "Ask me for more, Paddy."

"Please. More. I need more." He had no pride, not where Remy was concerned.

"Please, what?"

He didn't even have to think. "Please, sir."

"Perfect." Remy kissed him so hard he forgot to breathe, to think. All he could do was rock back and forth and feel.

Everything Remy gave him was huge, amazing, and every time his balls drew up, Remy tugged them away from his body, that and the leather keeping him caught. He thrashed, his body on the edge of the abyss, ready to fall.

"Not until I say. It may be hours."

"Hours?" His voice rose in alarm. He might die.

Remy's chuckle was pure evil. "Focus, Patrick. On now."

"I am!" He was burning up. The water would become steam soon.

"Can you feel your hole, stretched about me? Can you feel me filling you?"

He stared at Remy, his hunger so overwhelming that he could hardly speak.

"Into me, *bébé*. All of you poured into me."

"I can't. I'll disappear." Words poured out finally, but Patrick had no idea what they meant. All of his fears. All of his hopes.

"Never. I will see you until the end of time."

"Remy!" His body worked Remy's cock inside him, spasming as if he were having his little death, even if nothing issued from his prick, and Remy stole his breath, the kiss burning him.

His ears rang, his breath coming short, and then he heard Remy cry out, thrust deep, heat flooding him.

Patrick held the sides of the tub, and a strange happiness settled into him knowing he had given Remy this release.

Remy hummed softly, the thrusts becoming more and more slow.

Patrick gasped, his hands aching. "Remy, please."

"Mmhmm?"

Evil tease. The man was a rampaging danger to humanity. Patrick rocked his hips. "I'm dying. I am."

"No, *bébé*. You're needing." Remy stroked him again, nice and slow.

He shivered, his whole self buzzing with some sort of lightning in a bottle. "I am. I can't—"

Remy pulled free gently, then rinsed them both off. Remy stood, water pouring off him, so beautiful Patrick could barely look at him. "Come to bed, *bébé*. I will help you."

"You swear?" He stretched his legs, his hips screaming for a second.

"I do. I know just what to do next." Remy's eyes gleamed, that strong, lean body almost glowing in the lamplight.

"You steal my breath," he admitted.

"I want to steal your heart." The words made him glow, but he felt as if he knew nothing about the man Remy was, about his depths.

Worse than that, he felt as if he knew nothing about whether he had any depths of his own. He just… there was only so much he could remember.

"*Bébé*." Remy waited until he met his gaze. "Get out of the tub, Paddy, and come to bed. Now."

He stood immediately, not even stopping to dry off before padding to the bed, and Remy nodded to him with approval. He thought he ought to be disturbed by this, but somehow he couldn't manage it.

Instead, he felt a part of something for the first time in his life. Something only his.

Something true.

He reached out, cupped Remy's cheek, thumb rubbing the sharp angled jaw.

Remy nodded, kissing his thumb. "On the bed. Hands over your head."

His need was such that he followed, almost eagerly. Lord have mercy on his soul, but he needed Remy's touch. He lay back on the bed, pushing his arms up by his ears, gripping the bedposts.

"Stay there," Remy ordered. Then Remy went back to that bag he'd brought in, coming up this time with leather straps padded with fur.

"Remy?"

"Shh. Stay where I put you, *bébé*."

Technically, he had put himself there, but he really didn't want to argue. He burned with curiosity to know what would happen next. Dampness soaked into the sheets beneath him, his wet hair curled around his ears.

Remy joined him on the bed, kneeling by his chest. One of the straps dropped to the ticking, but Remy wrapped the other about the bedpost, then Patrick's wrist.

He opened his lips to protest, but Remy shook his head, murmuring soft nonsense to him. His lips shut, his teeth clicking together behind them. When Remy leaned across him to close the other loop around his opposite wrist, he just stayed still, swallowing hard. The bed seemed to slide across the floor, squeaking as it moved, and Remy shook his head. "*Non, bébé. Ici.* Here."

"I— Do I do it, Remy? Do I make things fly about?"

Remy scowled. "What did I say, Paddy? Are you so ready to think of other things?" Remy slapped his hip, the sting immediate and shocking.

His eyes flew open and the chandelier sang, the crystals clanking together.

"Look at me, *bébé*." The growl made him snap back to Remy and what they were doing. "So stubborn when you're afraid. I told you not to be afraid. I am right here."

"It ain't right, to be afraid, to be a yellow belly."

"It's natural, love, but we're together. There's nothing to fear in this place."

Love. The word wiggled inside him, sent out tendrils of peace. He wanted to believe in it, so he did. He relaxed into the bonds and allowed Remy to have his way.

"There. There it goes." Remy smiled for him, hands beginning to roam his body, callused fingertips catching on the rough hair on his chest, under his arms.

The leather around his cock became firm, a solid grip. He grunted, shifting his hips to try for some relief.

Remy's chuckle danced on his nerves, but those wicked hands never moved toward his hardness. Torture. Pure torture, especially when Remy stroked his thighs, his hipbones, with the lightest touches. "Spread for me, *bébé*. Nice and wide."

The words made him blush, but he obeyed, his legs spreading like butter for a hot knife.

"That's it." Remy touched his stretched and swollen hole, the contact sending bolts of pleasure up his spine. "Sensitive, hmm? It makes your prick throb."

"It makes everything quake." He couldn't stop the words.

"Not everything, though. Just you and me."

"Yes." Patrick glanced at the chandelier, which was still. Oh, God. Good.

A sharp snap landed on his inner thigh. "On me."

"Yes, sir." His gaze flew back to Remy. Evil man.

"Good." This time the touch Remy gave him was gentle, a breathtaking little stroke.

He stared down at Remy's hand, willing it to touch his aching cock.

"In good time, *bébé*. You need to learn patience."

"I waited for you my whole life, Remy."

"Did you?" Remy petted his belly, following the trail of hair from Patrick's navel. "Everything I did led up to you. Everything I learned."

He wasn't sure what that meant, but the warmth in Remy's voice heated him. His body undulated, trying to get closer, to get more of Remy's heat, which was like the hottest day in August.

Remy tugged his damp curls that crowned his cock, pulling with a slow, steady tug that had his eyes rolling back in his head.

When those fingers finally danced across the head of Patrick's cock, he shouted, his ass cheeks clenching.

"Such need. Stay focused, now. On me. On my will."

"Yes, Remy. Yes, sir. Please."

"That's my good lad. Mine."

Patrick knew he should fight the designation, but he understood, he thought.

It pleased Remy, suited him to the bone. Pleasing Remy could become a life's pursuit.

Remy leaned down, tongue dragging over his slit. The sharp rasp over his flesh made his hips punch the air, and he strained, but his hands stayed tied.

"I will stop, if one thing moves, *bébé*. If you focus, think of me, I will not stop. Understand?"

He bobbed his head furiously. "I understand. I do. I swear!"

"Good. I want this so badly." Remy licked all around the head, then down until that hot mouth met leather. The sudden change of heat made him whimper, made him buck and roll.

His eyes burned, but Patrick kept them open by dint of sheer will. He wanted to see Remy suck him, needed to see those hungry lips wrapped around his need.

Remy licked again, then wrapped his mouth around the tip, sucking lightly.

Patrick whimpered, but he refused — flat out refused — to look away. He needed this, so he needed to focus on his lover.

"Mmm." Remy rewarded him with a low sound, one that went straight to his balls.

All he could do was pant and focus and feel. Not a thing more. Remy touched the binding on his cock, and he jerked, his breath stopping for a moment, it seemed.

"You'll not spend, *bébé*. You'll wait for my say so."

"You have my word." He wasn't sure he could with the leather on… And then Remy unlaced it, leaving him free. Now he really did have to rely on his self-control.

He almost sat up, but the cuffs pulled him up short, shocking him. The jolt to his muscles made him grunt.

"Pulls, no?" Remy licked him, lips closing on small sections of skin, teeth a delicate threat on the shaft.

"Yes. Lord help me, I need you."

Remy worked him, hand about the base of his cock, lips around the head. Up and down, hand and mouth met.

His eyes dropped closed and he moaned, his pleasure roaring through him.

Remy stopped. Just stopped cold, hand and mouth leaving his skin. When his eyes popped open, Remy was staring at him. Waiting.

"Did I do wrong?" He hadn't heard anything move.

"No, *bébé*. I wasn't ready for you to spend, and you were trying to." Remy had that implacable expression, the one that said they were nowhere near done.

"Forgive me. I've never ached so. Never."

"There is nothing to forgive, *lapin*. I wanted to give you time to come back to yourself a bit." Remy began to stroke himself, his cock rising once more.

His mouth fell open, and he groaned, licking his lips. So lovely. It stole his breath. Remy's skin gleamed from their bath, the deep, rich color such a contrast to the snowy sheets.

"Your eyes burn like ice, *bébé*."

"Like ice…" He was melted. Patrick had no idea which way was up or down and, every time he tried to move, he felt the tug of the straps around his wrists. "I want to touch you."

"Too bad." Remy slid close once more, touching his wrists. "I want to see you bound and straining."

He groaned at the words, tugging at the cuffs. His cock bobbed, slapping his belly, the tip so wet. Remy was mastering him with the tiniest gestures.

He moaned, mouth open as he licked his lips. He swore he could almost taste Remy's prick.

"Is that what you want, *bébé*?" Remy climbed him, holding to the headboard and straddling his hips, standing on the bed.

"Please." He knew it would drive his need, but he knew it would also soothe him, ease his desperation somehow.

Remy nodded, reaching down to grasp that long cock, then rub it against his lips. When he flicked it with his tongue, he tasted Remy and musk and soap. He wrapped his lips around the sweet flesh and began to suck, tugging rhythmically. His balls ached with each pull, and his fingers curled into fists.

Remy stroked his arms, his shoulders, the touches like a light massage. That helped and hindered, his skin tingling as the blood flowed back into his hands. Patrick felt as if a tornado twisted inside him, spinning, and the only things holding him onto the bed were his lover, his lover's will.

Remy began to thrust, hips moving languidly at first. No fair, when he wanted to go fast and hard.

"My choice, *bébé*." How could Remy be so sure, so cool in the face of this need.

"Mmmph." He would have spoken but Remy pushed

between his lips, deep into his mouth. He swallowed hard, his hips punching up, fighting to match Remy's thrusts.

Especially when Remy moved faster, fucking his face, making him blind with need. His balls drew up, tightening close to his body and Remy reached back like he saw, like he knew, tugging them low in their sac.

"Not yet. We're coming close, *bébé*. I swear."

He whimpered, as near to breaking as he'd ever been.

"No. No, you're doing so well." Remy stroked his hair. "I believe in you, Paddy."

No. No, he didn't think he was well at all. He wanted to scream. He wanted to rage. He wanted Remy.

He looked up at Remy, staring into jet eyes, and suddenly his tension eased, melted away as Remy drew him in and cradled his soul.

Remy was all he needed, and Remy would never let him fail, never let him be harmed. His protector.

Remy nodded. "And you are my own." Slipping free of his mouth, Remy moved back down until their cocks pressed together before kissing him deeply. He let himself sink into the pressure of Remy all around him. Even his breath was flavored with his lover.

Grabbing a handful of his hair, Remy rocked against him, the other hand bringing their pricks together, rubbing firmly. His eyes crossed and he fed Remy one wild cry after another.

"*Oui, bébé*. Together. When you feel me go over."

"Together. Together." Anything. Anything at all. He'd offer Remy his soul to find his climax.

Remy laughed, the sound low and unbearably sensual. "Careful, *bébé*. I might take it." That lean hand jerked them once, twice more. "Now!"

Then a sharp sting dug into the slit of his cock and he shot, his entire world emptying out of the tip of his dick.

"*Merde.* You're stunning." Remy arched, seed spraying over Patrick's skin in hot jets.

He blinked slowly, his entire body slumping, sinking into the sheets. Patrick felt as if he'd been in battle for hours, his muscles like mush.

Remy stayed close for a few moments, then the heavy weight lifted, disappeared, replaced by a cool, soft cloth dragging over his skin. Once he was clean, Remy unbuckled the straps around his wrists, allowing him to lower his arms. Remy rubbed his arms, using oil to ease his tremors.

"You learned your lesson well. There will be more, some more challenging than others, but you have learned this one well."

Patrick shook his head slowly, not understanding, but the truth was, the things Remy made him feel were worth any confusion.

"But you did. You are beautiful in this, in your submission."

"I don't know what that means, Remy."

"I know, *bébé.* You will. We'll talk about more soon, but some things are better learned without talking." Remy's voice poured over him like a drug, soothing him deeper and deeper into sleep. He blinked hard, fighting it as long as he could, but Remy petted and soothed until he slipped under like a man drowning.

He would dream of Remy. Patrick just knew it.

Chapter Sixteen

After a week of training with Patrick, Remy knew they would easily make the deadline imposed by the Colonel. His boy was responsive, focused, and needy.

Remy was quite in love with him already.

His lover was plugged and bound, kneeling beside him, head on his thigh as he read. Remy turned a page, his arm brushing Patrick's hair. He was coming to relish these quiet times, coming to love how Patrick relaxed into bondage and allowed himself to simply exist.

His boy was thriving, the sweet soul showing signs of honest, deep healing.

Remy smiled down at Patrick. This association was good for him, as well. He had never been one for selfless acts. Patrick made Remy want to be a better man. He intended to keep this one, God help him, no matter what the consequence.

He reached out to stroke Patrick's shoulder. "Are you thirsty, *mon doux?*"

"Yes, sir. Please. I am."

Remy closed the book and set it aside so he could take up a glass of water. He gave Patrick a sip, then another. He traced Patrick's lips, smiling as they opened.

Bending, he kissed Patrick's mouth. "Would you like to have supper in the member dining room tonight?"

"What if I cause a...problem?"

"I think we've learned we can deal with that." He saw the lines of worry on Patrick's forehead and stroked them away.

"What can we do to make it better?"

"Whiskey?" The soft tease hid the wealth of Patrick's worry.

"Now, *bébé*, why would I let you dull your senses? When you have so much to feel?"

"I have felt all things, haven't I?"

He chuckled softly. "Nonsense. We have barely begun to explore all our options."

Patrick's blue eyes widened, the color like a midday sky. "Sir? Are you serious?"

"I am always serious, *bébé*." He leaned down and offered Patrick an easy kiss.

Patrick strained up to meet him, but those strong arms were bound behind Patrick's back, leaving him unable to reach up. He slid his foot under Patrick's balls, jostling the heavy wooden phallus piercing his boy.

"Oh!" Patrick arched, his red, swollen nipples and cockhead things of beauty.

He reached down, pinched one swollen bud with a steady, firm pressure.

"Remy!"

"Yes?" He lived for those cries, for Patrick's submission, but he knew he needed to begin working toward sharing Patrick with the world.

"Aches."

"And you love it, *bébé*, don't you?"

"I do. More?"

"Not yet." Remy slid to the edge of his chair. "We should try something else first." The day had been quiet. Restful. Patrick was in a good state of mind for an experiment.

"Something else?" Curious man.

"Indeed. I want you to bring me that pitcher."

"Yes, sir. Untie me?"

"I don't think so, *lapin*. I think you need to find another way.

Do not break it, if you please."

"I don't understand. You want me to use my mouth?"

"No." He tilted up Patrick's chin. "You have another option, *mon doux*."

Patrick's eyes took on that wild, unbroken horse look, and the air between them became heavy, electric. Nothing in the room so much as tremored, however, save Patrick.

Perfect.

Perfect, and now it was time for Patrick to begin to take ownership of the power within him.

"I— No, sir. I can't. It happens when I'm upset."

"Try for me, *bébé*. Just try." He had no doubt of his lover. None. Now Patrick needed to believe as well, to understand that he had control. That this was no demonic force moving upon him, but a gift. A muscle.

Patrick swallowed hard, staring at him for a long moment. Then he turned to look at the pitcher. "I don't know how to make it happen, to wake the demon."

"Well, now." Remy smiled, sitting back on the chair so he could reach for his deck of cards, sitting on the table next to his book. "It's not a demon, love. It's a talent. Like my way with cards."

Patrick's eyes were caught as he began to move the cards through his fingers.

"I have more than just an affinity for the cards. I have a talent for them. They speak to me, *cher*. They tell me things. They tell me when to play and when to fold." He slid the cards into a fan, then back into a single stack. "Now you must learn your gift, your talent. Try for me. Call for the pitcher."

Patrick watched him, watched the cards. "I will try for you, I will, but I don't know how to… What if it is a devil? Tricking us?"

"I know things, *non?*" When Patrick nodded, Remy smiled.

"I know demons, *bébé*. They haunt the air where I come from. You don't have one."

"You swear it? I feel...I feel as if there is a dark space, a hole inside me."

Remy had no doubt that space was dug into Patrick by the bullet in his brain, no doubt at all, but he had no reason to believe that love or time would illuminate that particular darkness.

"I believe in you," was what he chose to say. He touched those swollen lips. "I adore you."

Patrick kissed his fingertips, whispering softly. "For you."

"For us. Bring me the pitcher, *bébé*."

Patrick closed his eyes, nodding, before opening them again to turn toward the pitcher. For long moments, nothing happened. Then it rocked gently back and forth.

Patrick moaned, the muscled body beginning to shudder, to sweat.

"Shh. Be easy, Paddy. There's no need to strain. Call it to you. Coax it."

"It's so heavy."

"Is it? Heavier than the bed? No, you moved that easily." He put his hands on Patrick's broad shoulders. "Breathe. In and out. Will it to me. Let me reward you."

Patrick watched him, inhaling deep, sucking in heavy breaths. Soon, though, the breathing evened out, the sweat drying on Patrick's upper lip.

"Good. Now try."

He looked up, surprised to see the pitcher heading toward them, shuddering mid-air. Remy bit back his cry of triumph, not wanting to distract Patrick and break the hold. They needed this tiny victory.

"Keep breathing, *bébé*. Keep calling, just as you are."

"Bring the pitcher to you."

"That's right."

The pitcher wavered a bit, but it came onward, finally landing in Remy's lap. He cheered. "La! Just so, *bébé*. Look at that."

Patrick's chest heaved, the pulse in the sweet throat throbbing. "Remy. I did it."

"You did!" He set the pitcher aside in favor of rewarding his love with more kisses, deep ones that burned. He pulled his *bébé* onto his lap, bouncing the sweet ass on his thigh, making Patrick feel him deep within.

"Oh…" Patrick moaned, head falling back. "Please."

"You need so beautifully. I intend to keep you, *bébé*."

"Even with the…this talent you say I have?"

"Even so. I'll tell you a secret, hmm? No one at Club Raven is without such a talent. We all have one, large like yours or small like mine."

"All?" Patrick searched his eyes. "But Remy, I've seen dozens of men. Can there be so many?"

Was that relief in Patrick's eyes?

"Every one. Canaan, for instance. He has a talent for finding things that need to be found, if you will." Canaan was much more than that, but he'd just gotten Patrick to stop talking demons, hadn't he?

His God-fearing man was not ready to understand the delicacies of such things. He knew, as Patrick grew to be part of the club, that he would learn and grow on the subject. But not now.

Now Patrick needed to understand he was not alone and that he could control this gift. The first lesson was done. The second well begun. Remy was pleased.

He reached down to jostle the plug in Patrick's ass.

"Remy…"

"Hmm?"

"I swear, you make a man insane."

Patrick had no idea. Still, he knew what his lover meant. "I have so many plans for you, *lapin*. So many things I want to try."

"I want to know, Remy. I want to know so much." The tentative words made Remy's entire body clench, made him tighten viciously. Patrick had always taken what he had given, but had not yet asked for anything beyond simple release.

"Oh, *bébé*. The things we can explore." He pushed in the fake cock, then pulled it out a bit.

"We...we can." Patrick swallowed, moving on him like he was riding.

"Yes. One of the members, the one who gave me your cuffs. And this." Remy pushed the plug once more. "He has more toys. So many more."

"More." Patrick was near mindless, body moving up and down, taking the wooden cock deep, begging for it.

"Indeed, *bébé*. So many ways to make you need. Will you wear another plug for supper? Will you sit for a meal, dressed and proper, full for me?"

Blue eyes flew wide but Patrick nodded sharply. "Anything."

"And if I invite friends to join us? What then?"

"I trust in you. Completely."

His Paddy honored him. Remy's rusty old heart swelled with it, the dusty recesses healed by his young lover.

"Then we'll compromise, hmm? A few friends dining here in our rooms. We'll put your evening kit on over this…" He rocked the plug, loving every shiver and shudder.

"Anything. Anything, Remy. Please. I ache."

"And you'll ache through our meal. I will reward you well after."

Patrick took one deep breath, then another. "Yes. Yes, sir."

"My perfect lover." He held Patrick's hips finally, stilling them. They needed to calm down now so he could ring for Daniel to find out who intended to dine in and invite a few friends to their supper. Then they would bathe and dress and be ready to entertain.

His eyes fell on the pitcher where it sat, next to his chair, and he had to smile. He had to.

They were making real progress.

He couldn't be happier.

Chapter Seventeen

Patrick stood, shivering in his newly pressed kit, the lawn undershirt rasping at his swollen nipples.

The servants were setting the table for supper, laying out six chargers and plates. Six of all the silver and all the glasses…

He wasn't at all certain he could do this.

"Of course you can, because I asked it of you." Remy's questing hand cupped his ass, rocked the phallus inside him.

Patrick went up on tiptoe, his breath huffing out. "Only because you told me you would reward me, Remy," he teased.

"I will, *bébé*. I will make sure that by tomorrow you will be alight."

As if he wasn't tonight. He was pretty sure he glowed with need. Patrick cleared his throat. "So, who is coming? Tell me about them."

"Isn't that cheating?"

"How?" He deserved to know how they would all be, who they all were.

"Oh, very well." Remy came about to straighten his white tie. "I invited two couples. I thought their similar circumstances would put you at ease. Joseph is a railroad man, and his lover Samuel is from your part of the world, I believe. Isaiah was in the navy, and his man is named Jean." Remy pronounced Jean in the French way, so that one might be from where Remy was.

"Joseph, Samuel. Isaiah and Jean. Joseph and Samuel. Isaiah and Jean." He repeated the names as his mother had taught him.

"Yes. They're good men. Talented." Remy winked at that, and he laughed.

"According to you, everyone here is." He could hardly credit it.

"It's true. Shall I tell or leave you to discover?"

"Tell me what I need to not embarrass either one of us."

"Oh, *bébé*, you can never embarrass me." Remy was so serious about that. "Sometimes Jean lapses into French. You have to gently remind him that the rest of you do not speak it. Isaiah injured his left arm in a boat to boat attack. It is missing below the elbow."

"Oh, that's a shame." He reached up, touched the back of his head, lightning zinging behind his eyes.

"Tsk. That's mine to touch. Leave it go." Remy took his hand. "Samuel was hanged, his voice sounds like death and he has scars, quite severe ones."

"What was he hanged for?" Patrick blurted. Hanged. Goodness.

"Sodomy, *bébé*. His doomed lover was not as fortunate as he."

Patrick's eyes went even wider, enough that they pulled at the corners almost painfully. "And yet he has another male lover?"

"Joseph was most insistent, *bébé*. Joseph, in fact, quite saved his life."

"Like you saved mine?"

"Did I do that?" Remy's sharp smile was back, but Patrick was learning that was a good thing. "I'm glad."

A knock sounded at the door, and Remy patted his ass, making him swear. "Get that, *mon doux*?"

He stuck his tongue out at Remy, making sure he was beyond reach before he did, then he answered the door, finding a massive man standing there, dressed with military precision, beard neat and crisp, one sleeve empty. Beside him in gaudy frippery stood a dark haired, pointed little man with snapping blue eyes and the look of one of the pirates in the picture book he'd had as a lad.

"Welcome, y'all. Please, come on in." Patrick stepped back to let them by.

The big man gave him a thorough inspection in the military fashion. "Good to meet you, lad. Isaiah McAlvoy."

"Patrick Daniels."

"Jean. Jus' Jean. I don't need no other name."

"Pleasure." What an odd little man. Patrick gestured to the table, where Remy had plopped down at the head. "Please, have a seat. Shall I ring for Daniel, Remy?"

"Please, *bébé*. Joseph will be here soon, I vow."

"Always early, me," Isaiah said with bluff good humor. "Naval precision."

"Bah." Jean rolled his eyes. "Obsession."

Isaiah caught Jean with a look. "Sit, lad."

Jean opened his mouth and Isaiah simply pointed to the chair.

To his surprise, Jean dropped into the chair with a thud, crossing his arms over his chest.

Patrick found himself suddenly unnerved, and he searched out his Remy, his true north. Remy smiled and held out a hand for him.

As soon as their skin touched, he relaxed, his shoulders coming down from around his ears.

"There. There, *bébé*. Jus' so."

Somehow he thought he ought to object to Remy calling him *bébé* in front of others, but he couldn't do it. It was what Remy called him.

The door opened, and another pair of men came through. These two didn't bother to knock. One was a dapper man, slender and short of stature, with dark hair and oddly light gray eyes. The other was lean and lanky, tall enough to fill the doorway. Patrick was sure that the man had eyes, hair, features, but all he saw was the necktie of scars.

He looked away, not wanting to make the man uncomfortable.

"Ah, Joseph. Samuel. Please, come sit."

"Sorry if we're late," the dapper man said. He must be Joseph. "Samuel had the damndest time choosing boots."

Samuel arched an eyebrow, but beyond that didn't say a word.

"Sit, sit."

"Joseph. Good to see you." Isaiah nodded, a smile splitting his beard.

"Hello, you old sea dog. Have you been well?"

"Good. I'm good. How goes the railroad business?"

"It's a challenge, but what isn't these days?"

"True enough."

Joseph glanced at Remy. "How are you, my friend? You've been cloistered of late."

"I've had a rather particular interest holding me."

Patrick's cheeks heated, and he wiggled, his ass cheeks clenching on the plug. Remy smiled at him and there was no question that Remy knew exactly what he was doing, what he was feeling. His fervent prayer was that no one else did.

A soft knock preceded Daniel, who slipped easily into the room. "Good evening, sirs. Would you like to start with an aperitif?"

They all agreed and a bottle was seemingly produced out of thin air, a violet elixir pouring into tiny crystal cups.

Remy offered a silent toast by way of raising his cup, and they all did the same. They drank it down, and Patrick wasn't sure if it was sickeningly sweet or perfectly lovely.

He did know it made his ears ring a bit.

"Hooeee." Jean shook his head. "That was somethin'."

"Oh dear God, he'll be gagged and bound before the night is up." Isaiah rolled his eyes, but there was a smile there.

Jean smiled, as well, a slip of an expression sent only to Isaiah. He felt like an intruder seeing it.

Patrick looked down at the table, forcing himself not to see anything, not to look.

Remy squeezed his hand. "No one has anything to hide here, *bébé*. Do you understand?"

He looked up, confused. Worried.

"He's right, lad." That came from Isaiah. "We're all friends here. No censure."

"Patrick is new to this — to the company of men, to the idea of talented men, and to our specific...predilections."

"Ah." Joseph nodded. "Well, welcome. I think you'll like it here."

"Thank you, sir. I appreciate it. I've learned many things since my arrival."

Jean chuckled. "I bet."

"Jean." Isaiah glared and Jean pouted. Clearly, this was usual behavior.

"Don' let the idjits get to you, boy. You jus' pay attention. Mister Remy here won't steer you wrong." Samuel's voice sounded like the grave, but somehow he made Patrick ease some.

"No, he would never do that. He's my angel."

"I hear you." Samuel gave him a look that he understood completely.

"You're from near to me, I'd wager."

"Fredericksburg in the Republic of Texas."

"Greenville."

"I know of it. Cotton country."

He nodded. Indeed. His entire life, before the army, was ruled by cotton. He had never been so glad to see the last of something in his whole life.

He met Samuel's eyes, stunned to see that they were a pure black, no color at all, and he leaned away, almost painfully shocked.

"He ain't but a spirit talker, now." That was Jean. "The ones that done been cursed, they look that way."

"Jean. That is enough." Isaiah snapped it, and Jean jumped. Now there was no pouting, only an apologetic look.

"Sorry, Samuel."

"Only the truth. I wear dark spectacles out. Most folks think I'm blind. Here, I ain't got to lie to no one."

"I meant no offense, not a bit." He had no room to judge.

"I know it."

"Not to worry," Joseph said briskly. "We must all learn each other's foibles."

"Indeed." Remy smiled, nodded. "In time. Now, supper."

Daniel stood nearby, waiting. No one had heard him return to the room. "The kitchen informs me the menu this evening is lobster salad or baked crab, lamb roast or turkey, and an array of side dishes and relishes."

"We'll have the crab and lamb, Daniel." Remy was always so very sure, so definite.

"My boy wants the turkey," Isaiah said. "Send up lobster and crab and he can pick at them. I'll have the lamb."

"And we'll have the turkey." Joseph smiled at Samuel. "Samuel is not fond of lamb."

"No? I would never have guessed it." Remy's smile was teasing, playful, but Patrick's attention was caught by the way the captain so casually called Jean 'boy'.

He didn't think it was an insult.

Patrick shifted in his seat, trying to work the plug into a more manageable spot. He swore Jean was watching him, was staring at him with a knowing look.

His cheeks heated almost painfully and he smiled a little, willing to share his awkwardness and laugh at it.

Jean's smile was like the dawn breaking on the horizon, and he blinked, stunned at the transformation from sulky and odd to smiling and beautiful. He sat there, stunned into silence for a long moment.

Daniel appeared once more, carrying a tray of breads and cold meats and cheese, which he placed on the table unerringly despite his blindness. "Would anyone care for wine? Coffee?"

"Wine all around, yes? No one has far to go." Joseph smiled at Samuel, at Remy.

"Something very dry," Isaiah agreed.

"I'll bring a selection, gentlemen." Daniel disappeared again, and Patrick blinked.

"Is he a ghost?"

Remy opened his lips, but it was Samuel who answered, in that odd voice. "Never ask questions about men here that you ain't ready to know."

Patrick pondered that, then nodded. Very well. He would keep that question to himself for a time.

Joseph gave him a small smile, then built a little pile of meat on bread. "Do you read, Patrick?"

"I do. I can do my figures as well."

"I've been reading to him while he attends me," Remy murmured. "It suits us."

"Ah. Well, I was going to offer access to my books, but you already steal too many, Remy."

"*Moi?* Never say so!" Remy feigned shock not well at all. In fact, his dark eyes danced with merriment. Remy picked up a delicate slice of cheese, layered it on a bit of toast, then fed it to Patrick with his fingers.

He opened his lips to the bite before he thought, his cheeks burning with a mix of shame and arousal.

The flavors on his tongue distracted him, and Remy's soft touch on his cheek helped calm him even more.

Samuel took a small plate and began building little bites, making half a dozen before offering Joseph the whole lot.

"Thank you, boy."

Samuel didn't seem the slightest bit shamed.

He glanced at Remy, who was watching him with a glittering gaze. Yes. He was learning his lesson, he thought. He had the sudden urge to beg a kiss, to make sure he was doing well.

One of Remy's dark eyebrows lifted and he raised his chin.

Remy closed the space between them to give him the kiss he wanted, just a light brush of lips, but it sent shocks all through him, his cock jerking in his trousers.

"Lovely," Jean hummed, the word making him shiver.

"He ain't bad." Samuel sounded almost like he was making fun.

Patrick shot Samuel a mock glare, and Samuel snorted.

"I think these boys are gonna get along," Isaiah murmured. "What do you think, gents?"

"They're both damn Texans, after all," Jean said.

"I found you in the gulf, boy. Don't try to pass yourself off as something exotic." Isaiah casually reached over to pinch one of Jean's nipples through his thin shirt.

"You don't find me exotic, *cher*? Not even when I came at you with a dagger in the night?"

"Oh, I didn't say you weren't my very favorite vice, boy."

Patrick watched them banter, the passion between them unbridled, obvious. He felt overheated, utterly bewitched by these sophisticated men and their play.

Remy touched the small of his back, catching his attention, distracting him and drawing him back into those dark eyes.

Patrick smiled, nodding. Focus. Believe in Remy.

"*Bon. Bon, bébé.*" The words were soft, meant only for him.

He basked in the glow for a moment, then decided to find a perfect morsel and feed it to his lover. The act felt desperately daring and made him breathless. He chose cheese, because he knew how Remy loved the softer stuff on toast, and held it to Remy's lips.

Remy's smile grew wide, dark eyes sparkling with pleasure as his angel opened up to him. The treat was nipped from his hand, Remy licking Patrick's fingers clean afterward.

That nearly pushed too far, but Remy backed away before he could become unnerved.

"Are you going to hang about after supper and play some cards?" Remy asked the other men.

"We would love to, assuming you swear not to cheat," Isaiah murmured.

"I do not cheat. I have an affinity for the cards." Remy put on a haughty expression.

He met his lover's gaze, then the other men's. "He is no cheat."

"I know, lad. Don't get all put out." Isaiah winked broadly, and he had to smile.

Patrick liked all of these men already. Even Jean, with his kohl-lined eyes and beaded beard.

"Dinner, sirs." Daniel wheeled in a cart with half a dozen covered dishes stacked upon it, making Patrick's mouth water. "Wine. There's a sweet, dry, and extra dry, plus coffee and milk."

So many options. He allowed Remy to choose the wine. He had tasted it so rarely in his life that he wasn't sure what to pick.

"A dry red for you, *bébé*. I think that will be a good place to start. If you hate it we can have coffee." Remy was good to him, always anticipating.

"I like the sweet," Jean murmured, winking and chuckling. "Goes right to my head."

"My *bébé* comes from a family of teetotalers. He has to learn his palate."

"Ah." Joseph lifted the glass of wine Daniel served him, sniffing at it. "I like very dry wine, but we all have different tastes. See what you enjoy."

Remy clapped his hands. "We should have a tasting, no? I

will ask Julian what he thinks."

"He loves a reason for a fête, eh?" Jean said, then the man winked at Patrick. "Any reason."

"Oh." Patrick had no idea what to say. He felt very gauche. Almost bumpkinish.

Samuel rolled his eyes. "He means Julian likes his fancy parties. Costume ones and ones with formal dress. Makes a man itch. I don't attend."

"You will if I require it, lad." Joseph's words were...not cold. In fact, not cold in the least, but sure and clean, like a blade.

Samuel inclined his head, something almost adoring in the gaze he landed on Joseph. "Yes, sir."

The tone of Samuel's voice made Patrick wiggle again, the plug maddening him. Goosebumps tried to rise upon his skin and the wine glasses tinkled and shuddered upon the table.

Remy put a hand over his. "*Mon doux.* Look at me."

"I'm sorry," he whispered. He wasn't trying to do it, wasn't trying to make it happen.

"No need to apologize," Joseph said quietly. "Just listen to your master."

"Master..." He called Remy *sir*. What did master mean?

Remy stared into him, and his heart stopped slamming his ribs. It didn't matter what it meant. Maybe that Remy was the master of Patrick's heart.

The thought made his cheeks heat, made him tremble but, this time, the glassware stayed put.

Remy nodded, as if that was that.

A soft chuckle drew his eyes to Samuel. "Ain't that just the way, friend? I'd be lost without Joseph. Dead and gone."

He didn't know what to say, how on earth to respond. This was beyond anything he'd ever known. He had been to suppers at home, of course. Barn dances and parties, church socials, but nothing so much as this. Nothing where men spoke so...so freely with each other.

Remy forked up a bit of meat to feed him, and that saved him the need to talk. He nipped it off the fork, the flavor satisfying and savory.

That seemed to be a signal to everyone and they began to eat, delicious morsels nipped off slick fingers, the scent of wine heady on the air. The clink of flatware on dishes and of murmured thanks were the only sounds for a bit. Patrick concentrated on Remy, who seemed determined to drive him mad with little touches and perfect tidbits of food.

The wine was sharp, tangy in his mouth, and it made the world seem distant, soft-edged. Not like the fever dreams the laudanum had given him. This was just a pleasant blur, something warm and deep. Remy reached over, lifted his chin and fastened warm lips over his, feeding him a scant swallow of wine from his mouth.

He licked his lips when they separated, glancing quickly at the other men. Somehow, Jean had ended up in Isaiah's lap, and they were kissing in a long, languid manner.

Remy chuckled. "I think they moved on to dessert, *bébé*."

"This is…" His mother would call it a den of iniquity. "I did not know there were places such as this upon the earth."

"Now you know. Are you shocked?"

"Yes." It would be ridiculous to pretend otherwise.

Remy's lips curled gently. "Is it bad?"

Patrick knew Remy understood. This wasn't bad or ugly, just strange and disconcerting.

"Only odd to me."

He thought it was Joseph who laughed at him.

Samuel grinned, an open, happy expression that surprised Patrick. "I thought I was gonna end up getting hanged again first time I saw what went on here."

"I can imagine." He didn't think he'd ever touch another man after he'd been caught, and there had only been a beating from his father's bullwhip, not a hanging.

"Joseph learned me better," Samuel told him. "This is a safe place."

"There, *bébé?* You see?" Remy put a hand on his thigh.

"I see. I hope I see." He wanted to belong here, to be among these men, but mostly with his Remy.

"I think you do. You've had a lot to learn." Remy's approval washed over him like a warm sunny day, and he basked in it a moment.

"*Vous avez toujours été comme ça? A clairvoyant?*" Jean asked, and Patrick looked to Remy, curious.

Remy just shook his head. "English, Jean. He was injured in a battle. That brought out his talent."

"My brother was killed." The words were immediate, as if from another man, but his lips moved.

Joseph perked up somehow, staring at him, then Remy. "We should talk, *ami,*" he told Remy.

"Certainly. Later?"

"Indeed."

"Did I misstep?" he asked.

"Not one bit, *bébé.*"

Daniel slipped into sight, then began clearing dishes. "Dessert tonight is buttermilk pie or coconut nest cake."

His mother's cook had made the finest buttermilk pie south of the Mason Dixon line and he hummed just from the memory of it.

"Buttermilk pie," Remy and Joseph said together. Samuel chuckled, so he must like it, too.

"We'll try the cake," Isaiah said. "My boy likes coconut."

Jean rocked his hips on Isaiah's lap. "So good to me."

"My pirate." Isaiah's grin was purely naughty. "He burns for the islands."

"I burn for you, *cher.* Always."

"Good." One big hand landed in a hard smack against Jean's buttock.

Patrick's eyes went wide and he looked away, mind whirling.

"Sweet lad you got there, but I reckon he's one of us, bone-deep." He wasn't sure exactly what Samuel meant, but there was no question that it was wicked.

"*Oui, ami.* I think he has much to learn and I cannot wait to teach him." He would have protested, but Remy's hand stroked his lower back, petting him. Distracting him.

"Such lessons." Samuel lowered his voice and leaned closer. "Relish them, Patrick. Every damn one."

He nodded, hoping that he had found an ally in this odd drover.

Joseph touched Samuel's arm. "Samuel very much understands where you are, Patrick. If you ever have need of him, just ring for Daniel and he can come spend some time."

Samuel offered him a smile, and this expression seemed more familiar now, less terrifying.

Patrick smiled back, feeling how it stretched his cheeks in odd ways. Did he laugh so little? "Thank you. I do appreciate it."

"La." Jean pouted dramatically. "No love for me."

"Like you ain't got enough love, pirate."

The two men shared a look, one that made Patrick burn with curiosity.

Isaiah had this huge, booming laugh that made Patrick think of cannons on a ship. "He has enough, I wager. If not from me then from some of the other lads." Isaiah grabbed both of Jean's ass cheeks now, lifting him for a smacking kiss.

"Captain Isaiah enjoys watching Jean be put through his paces periodically," Remy whispered, lips close to his ear.

Patrick jerked, his mind shying away from that even as his body seemed to think that was a very interesting idea, indeed. Jean was lovely; of course people would love to watch him. He wasn't all scarred like Patrick or Samuel.

"I have no wish to watch another pleasure you, Paddy. I am the one made to touch you."

The words burned through him like a wildfire. He jerked, his ass clenching over and over. He couldn't breathe, couldn't think, except to wish he wore the leather laces on his prick to keep from embarrassing himself.

The table spun once, and he forced himself to stop, to breathe and fasten his attention to Remy.

"That's good, *bébé*. So good." Remy gave him another kiss, one that went slow and deep and made his ears ring.

There were soft moans on the air, surrounding them, and Patrick thought he had felt more need in the last fortnight than in his entire life before. These men… they were not ashamed, so open. Loving. Patrick had to believe that was a good thing, no matter what his upbringing had taught him.

When Remy sat back, the table was back to normal, and desserts sat on dainty plates, the strong smell of coffee replacing wine.

Time passed so oddly here, and he found himself spinning from one amazing moment to another.

Remy reached down between his legs, palm pressing against his cock. "So you remember the night I took you to the dining room, *bébé*?"

"Yessir." He would never forget.

"Tonight we can be even more… free. Here we are all good friends. No one will care if we find our pleasure with dessert."

He wondered if that meant he was allowed to look. At the dining room he had only been able to see Remy. Here he might— There were so many maybes.

"You can look your fill, feel all you wish. This is our space, our place, you understand?"

"I hope so." If he didn't, he was a newborn fool. He glanced at Joseph, who had moved closer to Samuel, hand on Samuel's back. Jean and Isaiah, well, Jean straddled his big boat captain now, his arms around Isaiah's neck.

"I vow you do." That hand kept moving, pushing and rolling against his placket.

"Remy." Nothing shook, though. Nothing tremored but him.

"*Oui, bébé?*" Remy was fixin' to drive him out of his mind.

"I need more." He was supposed to ask for what he wanted. Remy had said so.

"More of what?"

A low chuckle made him glance again at Samuel, who was sliding off his chair and onto his knees on the floor.

Oh, sweet Jesus, look at that. He nearly spent.

"What do you want, *bébé?*" Remy opened his placket, slipped one button at a time.

"You." More than anything, he wanted Remy's touch, Remy's attention.

"That's the best answer, *mon doux*. The very best." Remy pulled out Patrick's cock, the air almost unbearably cool on his heated flesh. He was rigidly hard, sweating, and out of the corner of his eye he could see Jean's now-bare ass.

Jean draped himself over Isaiah's legs, naked and offered up like a sacrifice.

A sharp slap sounded, Isaiah raising his hand and bringing it down against Jean's skin. The way Jean moaned spoke of pleasure, not pain.

"Remy?" he whispered, utterly shocked and terribly intrigued.

"Jean needs discipline, *bébé*. You see how he acts out, begging for Isaiah to give him what he requires." Remy waved his free hand at Samuel, who had wrapped his mouth around Joseph's surprisingly large cock. "Samuel, he's more interested in serving Joseph's desires."

"And what do I need, then?"

"Focus. Control. You need someone to help take you out of your worry." Remy looked fierce for a moment. "That is my job."

A job? Was this a chore for Remy or a calling? Oh Lord.

Remy lifted his chin. "Paddy. On me."

"Yes." On Remy.

"I burn for you, Paddy. Never doubt that." Remy stroked his cock, then pressed his thumb hard against the slit. His gasp sounded loud in his own ears.

He jerked, eyes wide. "I— hands behind my head?"

Remy's eyes flared, gold ringing the dark. "Yes, *bébé*. That would please me."

He whimpered softly, caught in that gaze, his hands rising of their own accord. He fastened his fingers together behind his neck, his arms bulging a little with effort.

Reaching up, Remy pinched his left nipple, twisting it under his shirt, tugging hard enough that he swore he felt the weave of the fabric, each separate thread. His cock jumped in Remy's other hand, his hips rocking.

"My needy *bébé*. You wear the little aches so well."

"I do?"

"You do. It's not the grand pain, like Jean over there. It's the scratches and bites, the stretching and plugging." Remy's finger pressed hard against his slit, the burn enough to make him grit his teeth.

His ass cheeks worked the plug, his thighs feeling as if they were stone. A soft moan drew him, and he glanced over to find Joseph watching them, one hand in Samuel's hair.

Oh, dear God. He was doing this with other men, at a supper tab…

"Paddy." Remy slapped his cock with a flat palm.

He jumped, but he nodded. Yes. Bring him back to just Remy. Patrick loved Remy. He knew it now, knew he would do anything for this man he called sir.

Remy began to spank his cock — not hard enough to hurt, but hard enough to ache, to begin a steady burn that seeped into his balls. He understood now, what Remy meant about Jean. About what he needed, and how Isaiah gave it to him. It worked both ways.

His eyelids grew heavy as the blood pooled in his prick, the clear drops of need slipping from the tip.

Remy gathered them, the touches too soft after the slapping. He shivered, watching as Remy licked his fingers clean.

"I do love the flavor of your need, *bébé*."

"Kiss me? Please, Remy."

Remy slid off his chair, climbing into Patrick's lap. He'd seen Jean do just this to Isaiah but with Remy it seemed predatory, not supplicating. Remy pressed him down, surrounded him.

The kiss he got scorched him. His lips pressed back against his teeth, and Patrick tasted blood. He gasped, the lights in the room seeming to dim as he bucked up under Remy's weight.

Remy bit his lower lip, fingers digging into the backs of his wrists. "More."

"More?" He jerked up, rocking into Remy once more.

"Yes. I want you mad for me, *lapin*. Begging. I want you." The words came with more biting kisses, more pressure.

"You have me." He pondered. "May I use my hands?"

Remy shook his head. "Keep them where they are, *bébé*. I need access."

"I—Yes, sir." He leaned back as much as he could in the chair, letting Remy have his whole front. The plug slammed into him and he cried out, his ass on fire.

Remy's chuckle seemed to make the light flutter, the candles gutter.

"Damn, boy." Isaiah was grunting, Jean turned to face him now, riding his lap.

"Don't stop, Samuel. Take me." Joseph's command was sure, firm. Wicked.

He looked back to Remy, who watched him like a hawk, those eyes so dark, so unavoidable. Remy touched his hot cock again, rubbing just about the head.

"Such need, such passion, in this sweet cock."

"Yes. For you." He strained, begging with his body. Patrick would use his voice soon.

"I may have to embed a ring here, to remind you to focus."

The thought slammed through him, and the lights went out, the candles snuffed, the oil lamps dark.

A short, sharp laugh sounded, and he thought maybe it was Jean. "Oh, the things we do in the dark, *mes amis*."

Definitely Jean.

"Now, *bébé*, we need light. Light them up again." Remy seemed to think that was perfectly reasonable to ask.

"Do I know how?" There was the barest ember and he told it to become a flame, to grow, to feed.

The lamp lit first, flaring toward the ceiling before going back to a simple burn.

"*Oui!* Beautiful."

He panted, his eyes rolling back in his head as he tried again, tried to please. He strained to just light the candles, not burn them to ash.

"Easy. Easy, *bébé*. Control will come."

"Promise?" He laughed a little, feeling light-headed.

"I give you my word." Remy pinched his nipple again and two of the candles flared to life.

"Look at that, Samuel. Just look." Joseph sounded so pleased, and he thought it was for him.

"That's a powerful gift, Master. Damned. They'll be hunting him, they ain't careful."

"Mmm. We'll have to help, hmm?"

Patrick looked to Remy. What did that mean?

"Shh. Don't you worry. You are among friends."

"I want to make you proud." He wanted Remy to need him, to desire him.

"You make me so much more than proud, *bébé*." Remy kissed him again, shattering his thoughts, his worries.

He danced under Remy's body, trying not to spend, his clothes scratching at him, his arms shaking.

Remy rested their foreheads together, dark eyes gleaming at him. "I will have you marked here, beringed." Remy pinched the tip of his prick, then his nipples. "And here."

"I—" His breath caught, his body shaking right there on the edge. "I can't hold on, Remy."

"We're among friends, *bébé*. Let your need go. Come for me."

He shouted, because the release ached, his balls so tight to the base of his cock he couldn't stay still. His ass clenched on the fake phallus, and he wished it was Remy's real prick.

"Soon. Soon you can ride me into the very ground, *bébé*." Remy's fingertips dug into his hips.

"Yes. Oh, please." Now he was begging. He'd spent so hard his ears rang, but he was still begging.

"You have my word. I will give you my cock, fill you up with me until you know nothing else."

"Remy." He panted, his hands clenched so tightly they tingled from lack of blood.

"*Bébé*." Remy kissed him, then drew one of his hands down, giving him leave to touch.

He swallowed hard, licking his lips. Then he undid Remy's buttons, one by one, baring the perfect skin to his touch. His mouth watered, and he wasn't sure what to do. Suck Remy like Samuel had Joseph. Or beg to be fucked like Jean.

He fished the heavy cock out and began to pet the thick shaft. The heat astonished him, the scent of musk meeting every tug. Remy rocked on his thighs, moving like a band was playing a waltz.

His cock began to rise once more, astonishing him. His Remy could raise a dead man.

"Don't stop, *bébé*. Make me need it."

He nodded, tugging at Remy's prick over and over. Remy needed him; he held the evidence in his hand, and it was a thick promise, a heavy club of heat. He wanted to taste it, wanted it inside him any way he could get. Patrick lifted Remy, rising from the chair and spinning around. He sank to his knees, just as Samuel had, pushing his mouth over Remy's heated flesh.

"*Bébé!*" Remy arched and pressed deep and Patrick could feel the rush of arousal everywhere, pressing into his skin, into his skull. This was what he lived for, where he knew he was safe. With Remy, this way, nothing could harm them. Need seemed to flow between them, the pleasure crashing like a wave.

He barely heard the increased moans and groans from the other men, but they added to the heat in the room, the pressure. Patrick went down as hard as he could, swallowing around the base. Remy's fingers tugged at his curls, moving him, directing him.

He licked and sucked, bobbing, his tongue and lips working. Patrick pushed his hands back behind his head, knowing Remy would approve. In fact, Remy's cry was wild, one of pure need and all for him.

Patrick worked, his cock rigid once more, his ass wagging back and forth, the plug scraping and pushing at him.

He wanted to touch himself, to stroke off, but he didn't. Patrick would wait. Focus. Remy would tell him when it was time.

Focus.

On Remy. Always on Remy.

"*Oui. Oui, bébé.* My perfect one."

Perfect. No, but he loved with all he had. He bobbed faster, wanting to taste his lover's seed.

Remy's fingers tightened, then the cock in his lips swelled, pushing his mouth wider. He clamped down with his mouth, knowing he was about to get his reward. Remy poured into him, the salt coating his tongue.

Swallowing convulsively, Patrick took down every drop, not willing to lose a bit. The flavor of Remy was a drug, making him pull harder, beg for more.

Remy touched the back of his head, the contact with that… divot? Whatever. It made him shudder.

The caress came again and again, and lightning flashed behind his eyes, the world spinning. Patrick felt faint, swoony, as if he was having those vapors his mother spoke of.

"Focus, *bébé*. On me." Remy's voice seemed to come from so far away and he forced his eyes open.

On Remy. He licked the tip of that fine cock, then stared up into Remy's eyes.

"Good. Good. So proud. Stay with me, hmm? Stay right here."

"Here with you." He nodded, unable to look away.

Remy tapped his skull again and there was a pop from the table as one of the pieces of stemware snapped.

"No." Remy barked out the word. "Paddy. This is you and me. Nothing can hurt you."

"My brother…"

"He's gone. This is you and me." Remy tapped again.

Patrick closed his eyes. His brother. His brother had died. Everything shook, inside and out.

"Boy." Remy's voice brooked no resistance and he opened up, stared into blackness. "Where are you?"

"Here."

"And who are you with?"

"You, sir. I'm with you." I love you. He knew it. He loved Remy so much.

"Then trust me. Trust me, Paddy. Just stay here."

He nodded very deliberately, feeling Remy's fingers on his scalp. "I am. Here."

"Excellent." Remy sounded so pleased.

"He died. I was hurt." The words sounded misshapen and odd.

"You were. Here. A bullet. Right here." Remy tapped again, the world spinning.

"No."

"No?" Remy hummed, then rubbed that spot one more time. "Oh, *mon doux*. You amaze me."

"It's a hard thing, to know when you've slid on the other side of death," Joseph said, voice barely audible.

Samuel reached out and touched Patrick's shoulder, the contact shocking and warm and quite comforting. "Welcome back, Patrick. To the living."

It should have been Henry. Really, Henry should have lived.

Remy lifted his chin, dark eyes fierce. "No. None of that. You are mine, and you live now. You hear me?"

"Yes sir." Had Remy heard him? How?

"Good." Remy kissed him so hard he couldn't think of anything, let alone his past.

He was drawn back into Remy's arms, cradled and rocked, and when he came back to himself, they were alone. He wasn't sure how his lover did that, make time itself something slippery.

Patrick wasn't going to complain. Especially not when Remy pulled him to his feet and took him to the bathing area. He was only vaguely aware of Daniel clearing out the dishes and table, but Daniel was his friend. Wasn't he?

He thought so.

There was a bath drawn, the water steaming gently, the oil in the water scented with musk.

"Someone loves us, hmm?" Remy undressed him, then slipped the plug free from his backside. He gasped with the sudden emptiness, his knees going weak. "Shh. In the tub, *bébé*. You did so well."

He slipped into the water, hissing as the sting buzzed along his skin.

"You worked hard, *lapin*. That was an amazing meal." Remy did sound pleased, proud. Those lean, warm hands washed him gently.

"Thank you. I wanted to make you proud."

"You make me happy in every way, Patrick. Never doubt it."

He leaned back in the tub, and he blinked slowly, focused on nothing but the drag of the cloth on his skin. His muscles relaxed, and he melted into the warmth and care Remy gave him. Nothing else mattered. Nothing.

"Mmhmm. Just so, *bébé*. Just so."

He looked into Remy's dark gaze, getting lost. "Stay with me."

"I would no more leave you than I would cease breathing, *bébé*."

He caught Remy's hands with his. "Thank you. Thank you, Remy. I would be dead without you."

Remy kissed each of his hands in turn. "You're mine, Paddy. I would walk through hell for you. And you are doing a fine job of being alive. Just fine."

"I hope so." He wasn't sure, but he was willing to try.

He was happy, strangely enough. He'd never been that at home. Not ever. Not even riding the pastures, not even with Henry.

Remy slid into his arms this time, as if his lover needed comfort as well. He held on, the water lapping at them. Patrick wrapped himself around Remy and decided he didn't care what happened tomorrow. Not right now.

This was all he could possibly need.

Chapter Eighteen

Patrick slept the sleep of the innocent and righteous, his eyelids looking bruised, he was so exhausted.

Remy, though, he couldn't sleep. He rang for assistance, either Daniel or Anek, perhaps, someone who would watch over his boy. So to speak.

Daniel appeared almost instantly. He seemed to have taken a real interest in Patrick, and Remy wasn't going to complain. Daniel was a solid, steady presence. "I think I need to seek a game of cards, Daniel. Can you alert me if Patrick wakes?"

"Immediately, sir, but he will not wake until you return."

He did adore Daniel, genuinely. Remy smiled and nodded. "Thank you, *mon ami*." He grabbed a deck of cards and his wallet, which was still stuffed from his last game outside the club. Really, he needed to get out and about with Patrick.

He needed to take Patrick home soon.

Something that Samuel had said niggled at him.

"That's a powerful gift, Master. Damned. They'll be hunting him, they ain't careful."

No one was taking his Patrick from him. He needed to teach Patrick to use his gift deliberately. They were doing well, but time was short.

When he made his way to the gaming room on the second floor, the one only certain members attended, he found Lionel James, Isaiah and Jean, and owner Julian playing whist.

"Is there room here for another?" he asked.

"Of course, my friend. Sit with us." Julian's clipped English accent always made him smile.

Jean shot him a smile. "I liked your boy, eh?"

"Did you?" Pleasure warmed him. "I think you and he and Samuel can be fast friends, *chou*."

"*Oui*. He would have been a bad pirate. Those are always the bes'."

"He would have, no? He's far too honorable." He plopped down in a chair, noting Julian staring at him. "What is it, *cher*?"

"He's pushing a lot of energy into the ether, Remy."

"But it's better already." Remy leaned forward, even if earnestness was not his strong suit.

"His control is good, friend, for someone so new, with so much raw power." Isaiah was a good man, a good friend.

Jean nodded. "He's a little addled, no? The bullet?" Jean pointed to his head. "Remy's done got him, tho'."

"You have a pair of champions," Lionel murmured. Lionel was a powerful man, his talent for reading people hard to beat.

"I won't desert him, Julian. He's a good man."

"He's powerful. A beacon in the darkness," Julian muttered.

"I know." Remy shook his head, picking up the cards Isaiah dealt him. "He'll be ready to go home with me in a week, maybe less. I swear. We'll keep the darkness at bay."

"He'll be back, though? He's going to be fun to play with, *cher*." Jean was a wicked man.

"We'll be back often." He knew Patrick would need his friends, including Jean and Samuel, and yes, even blind Daniel. He'd require a good deal of reassurance, especially at first. The world outside could be... loud, and sometimes his beloved would need that original room, the heady focus and silence it would afford.

"And sometimes he'll need to know there are other wicked lovers of men out there," Lionel murmured, mouth curving in a smile that spoke of pure deviltry.

"Never say so," Julian said, face carefully blank.

Isaiah hooted. "Well, this is the place for that, certainly. Thank you for supper, by the by. It was educational and quite tasty."

"I wasn't aware you had anything left to learn, you old sea dog."

"Oh, my boy always has something to teach me." Isaiah reached over to pinch Jean's ass, which had to be sore from the long spanking he'd received.

Jean didn't even wiggle, but the wicked smile got wider.

"Now, lads, we're playing whist." Julian's smile seemed strained. He did seem to be lacking for company of late.

"We are." He looked at Julian, hoping for a hint as to how to ease his friend's worry, but there was nothing.

Lionel reached over, placing a hand over Julian's. "It will be all right, Jules."

"Of course it will. Play your cards."

Lionel laughed. "We need to find a new boy."

"What happened to that juicy little Horace fellow you had, Lionel?"

Lionel wrinkled up his nose. "He was a dear lad, but he had no interest in my more perverse desires."

"That's a shame, *M'sieu* Lionel. You're a legend of perversity." Jean was the worst kind of tease, he swore.

Lionel laughed, then got them all playing again. "Indeed. There's no shortage of young men who want to try me."

Remy understood that, but he found himself reluctant to try another for now. In fact, Patrick inspired him. He wanted to be with his lover for good.

"I think Remy is like me, my friends. Paired up."

"It's the end of an era, *cher.*"

"Whatever will poor Canaan do when he comes to town?" Julian murmured.

"Watch." Jean laughed, throaty and happy. "He do love to watch, that one."

"True enough." He thought Canaan might be the most wicked of them all. Maybe Canaan was one of those demons Patrick feared. It wouldn't surprise him at all.

"Are we playing for pin money?" Lionel asked.

Remy shook his head. "Not with you at the table, my friend."

Lionel offered him a patently false expression of shock.

Isaiah snorted. "No one in this place would ever believe that, friend."

"No?" They all began to chuckle, all but Julian, who simply watched with a fond expression.

Sometimes Remy wondered at the men who owned the Club. What terrors they must have seen.

There was something deep within, something outside the purview of a mere gambler. He shook his head, because Julian's gaze had sharpened on him, and he didn't want to upset the man anymore.

The cards called.

The only whisper louder in all the world seemed to be his Patrick.

No one had ever beaten the cards.

As if Remy had summoned him, he heard Patrick in his mind, querulous, wondering where Remy was. He heard Daniel soothing his boy, just singing an old song, soft and sweet. Patrick lapsed back into sleep, and Remy played another round.

He needed this time.

He needed the low murmur of friends, of the game. When Samuel and Joseph joined them, freshly scrubbed and smiling, Remy relaxed fully, basking in the warmth of good friends.

Samuel didn't join the game. He sat, silent and watching, black eyes like marbles. Remy had been unnerved by him at one time, but now he knew Samuel well, and understood his pain.

More than that, he respected the things those unnerving eyes saw. Samuel was one of those who stood on the front lines of assuring the Raven's securities held.

Samuel turned to glance at him, a small smile popping up. "I like your boy."

"Thank you. So do I. I told Jean, I hope you'll be friends."

"We will. You'll not be able to keep him here, permanently. They will feed off him. He's a beacon and, in this place, he echoes."

"No. No, I expect to take him home in less than a fortnight." He wanted Patrick to see his home, to wander the halls and wonder at all the strange things Remy had found in his travels.

"Good. I reckon I'll visit often, with my master's say so."

"I hope so."

Joseph chuckled. "I hope so, as well. I would love to come over as well, should I be asked."

Remy winked broadly. "You know you're all welcome. Well, save Lionel," he teased.

Lionel threw his head back and laughed. "You just don't want me to see your collection of dolls or something, eh?"

"I have a vast array of the poppets for the Voodoo, eh?"

Jean made the sign of the evil eye.

Julian rolled his eyes. "Amateurs."

"You ev' be in the sight of one of them, M'soo?" Jean looked horrified. "They take you soul, I swain."

Lord, the more riled Jean became, the less he could be understood.

Isaiah laid a hand on Jean's shoulder. "He's had a few bad experiences. Calm yourself, *amour*."

Jean settled immediately, pushing into the touch like a huge cat.

Oui. Soon that would be how Patrick responded to him. Remy knew it, deep in his heart. They'd come so far already.

Isaiah caught his eye, winked at him. Perhaps he was not hiding his thoughts as much as he ought. Then again, at Club Raven it was difficult to hide anything. These men knew things.

He supposed he knew things as well.

"Play, Remy, before we kick you out of the game." Julian's silvery eyes settled on him, laughter lurking there now.

"Blasphemy." He played, then took the hand easily.

They all laughed, Joseph making some remark about the inevitable. He did love the cards, and they returned the favor.

Everyone had their talents, after all.

Well, at least everyone at the Club Raven.

Chapter Nineteen

Patrick set his teeth and headed out of their rooms, determined to be able to explore on his own.

Remy seemed to understand, waving him off from where he was nursing a headache after a late night of cards and cups. "The library is simply two left turns and then three doors. If things begin to seem odd, ring for Daniel."

"I can do that." He'd been about with Remy a few times now, to visit with Isaiah and Jean, and to go once more to the private dining room. He knew where the bell ropes hid.

There was a heavy copper bracelet about his wrist now, a constant presence that reminded him that he belonged to Remy, that he had someone to focus upon. Patrick rubbed it with the fingers of his opposite hand, smiling. Focus.

Left turn. Left turn. Three doors.

The door was heavy, dark and banded with copper. Was this it? Was this right?

He knocked, and the door swung open.

The fact that no one was there to open it might have scared him at one time. Now he knew better.

Patrick expected the room to look dusty and scholarly. Instead, it was a grand, tall room with laddered shelves and leather chairs and divans, reading nooks and library tables.

He walked in, trying not to feel uncomfortable, not to look like the foreigner he was.

A familiar face appeared when Samuel stood, smiling at him. "Well, howdy, Patrick."

"Samuel. Hello." Oh, thank God. "How are you today?"

"I reckon I'm better now. Come have a sit."

"Thank you. Remy reads to me, and he wants me to find more books, but I think he really wants to see if I can be out on my own." He chuckled, sitting across from Samuel.

"This place can be a challenge for new members. I once thought I'd never leave our rooms. Never."

"Really?" Patrick straightened his shirt cuff. "Do you live here? At the club?"

"I do. Can you imagine me, out there? Wandering around Baltimore with these eyes?"

"I haven't seen the city." He shrugged. "I reckon my daddy would hang you for a demon, though."

"Already been done and Death decided not to take me. I saw him, looked into his eyes, and he walked away from me."

Patrick shivered. "I suppose so." He didn't know what else to say. He liked Samuel just fine.

Samuel snorted for him, that scarred throat working. "Shit, honey, you don't have to make small talk. We can just sit together and bullshit."

"Oh." His cheeks heated at the *honey*, but he was glad as hell he didn't have to pretend to know how to be polite and all. "I didn't know how to be social before Henry—" His head ached for a moment. "Before."

"Your brother?"

He nodded. "My twin. He was the better of us."

"Well, now you're the only one of y'all, huh?"

He nodded, the spot on the back of his head throbbing painfully. "They want me to marry his girl."

"Good thing you left, then. You got Remy now, and he won't let no one take you. I never seen him take a shine to anyone like he has you."

"I don't even remember traveling here. Nothing. It's like another life altogether."

"I know that one." Samuel raised one hand and touched his throat. "I came here half dead, I think. Maybe more than. All I know is if it wasn't for Joseph, I'd be a goner."

"Did someone bring you to him? Like me?"

"I think it was the same man, honey. Canaan."

"He was a friend of my father's."

"He is whatever he needs to be."

Patrick shook his head. "There seems to be a lot of that here." He leaned forward. "Daniel is a ghost, isn't he?"

"He is."

"Why can I see him?" He believed that spirits existed, but he'd been raised to believe seeing them was a sin.

He'd been raised to believe a shitload of things were a sin.

"Because he wants you to. Some folks never see him."

"I'm glad he does, then." He chewed his bottom lip. "So do you see them a lot? Spirits?"

"Yep." So blunt. Samuel just said it baldly, as if it was normal. "You want to ask me something, you ask."

"Is Henry...is he with me? You'd know, he looks just the same as I do." He wasn't sure if having Henry close by would be a pleasure or a horror.

"No, honey. Your brother may or may not have moved on, but he ain't with you." Samuel reached out to touch his wrist.

"Oh, thank God." He didn't know that he'd be relieved until the crushing emotion flooded him. He didn't want to live under Henry's shadow anymore.

"There you are, honey. It's just fine." Samuel's ruined voice shouldn't sound comforting, but it did.

"I just..." He didn't want to have someone hanging around him, waiting for him to err.

"Hell, if anyone can understand it's me, Patrick." Samuel laughed, a sound like someone gargling acid.

"I reckon." He couldn't imagine how frightening it was, to

see people that...well, he couldn't say they weren't there, because they obviously were. Daniel was there, was a real person, real enough to touch, to serve supper.

He considered Daniel a friend, in fact.

"Tell me about the club, Samuel." Patrick wanted to understand more.

"What do you want to know?"

"Everything? What is this place? Why is it here?"

Samuel pondered that, pursing his lips. "It's a big old haunted house, I reckon. It has an energy of its own, and all of us try to keep it in balance."

"Why not just...bless it?" Did it work that way?

"Too big. It was here before there were buildings." Samuel shrugged. "You'd have to talk to that Giles feller to really get the history."

"I'd rather just talk to you." Talk to someone who understood him.

"Well, I'll tell you anything I can, honey."

"Do you like it here?"

"I do. I have my Joseph, you know?" Samuel chuckled. "I got some good friends. It's different outside these walls. I cain't walk about like most. People stare."

"I'm sorry." He'd stared too.

"Even Joseph stared at first. It's weird. I cain't see it so much. When I look in the glass I see my old eyes. They was blue."

"Like mine?" He tried to imagine that, the vision of his newly made friend with light eyes.

"Yep. Maybe a little darker." Samuel laughed again. "You want somethin'? Maybe some coffee and cake? We can go on down to the dining room and I can bring you back up for a book."

"Surely. I'll get the hang of this place eventually. I know I will." He had to. He needed to learn how to wander about, find things.

"You will. It changes itself to disconcert you." Samuel held his hand when they left the room, humming easily.

"But why? I'm not threat to anyone."

"Oh, honey, it does that to all of us. We learn to just walk where we know to go. The more you let it move you, the more it will." Samuel led the way to the private dining room.

"Walk where we know to go." For whatever reason, the words made him smile.

"Yes. You see, now that I've brought you to the dining room, you know how to get here. You just gotta trust that you know, not look at things real close."

They sat, Samuel ordering chocolate and cakes from a slight, pale wisp of a man, before Patrick leaned forward. "Before, when I was lost, there were paintings here in the hallways. Wicked paintings unlike anything I've ever seen."

Ever dreamed.

Samuel's mouth curved, that smile anything but angelic. "Now, those you ought to study, my friend."

"Samuel, I couldn't imagine such acts."

"I bet Remy could, honey. You might want to start." Samuel winked. "My Joseph probably painted some of them."

He knew that he was gaping like a landed fish.

"What? He does fancy himself an artist, and he ain't bad. I think he used to work at a bank as some high mucky muck, but then I came along." Samuel grabbed a cookie off a plate placed before them. "Now he's kinda stuck here."

"If he did them, they are...not poorly done, but the subject matter would not be well-met." Especially not the one with the man with his... He couldn't even think it.

"Yeah?" Samuel gave him a knowing look. "Which one did you like best?"

He shook his head, but then muttered. "There was a couple. A few. You know."

"Mmmhmm." That chuckle was positively evil. "You tell me yours and I'll tell you mine."

"The one with the man's hand...Samuel, is that even possible?"

"Inside?" Samuel whispered and he swallowed hard, Adam's apple bobbing. "Hell, yes. Hell, yes."

His body went hard, hot, and he whimpered softly, shifting in his chair. For a second, he wished the wooden plug filled him, spread him.

Samuel cleared his throat. "Jean told me about it, and I told my Sir there was no such thing. He proved me wrong."

"Could you walk the whole week after?"

"Bowlegged for a few days, for sure."

Patrick had to chuckle. Had to, because there was no other way to hide his arousal. "And your favorite?"

"There's one with a man all bound up, his cock hid away, riding a fat prick screwed right into the floor while he sucks his Sir off. That one, Joseph painted it for me."

His cheeks flamed, but Samuel was so open, so honest that he deserved the same. "Remy has bound and plugged me. I find it excruciatingly arousing."

"Ex-cer-ushiatey, huh? You must have schooling."

"I do. Too much. I didn't want to be a rich man with his coffers. I was always running off when I was supposed to be doing lessons."

"Mmm. Well, there are some perks to my Sir being a rich man, I got to tell you."

"I saw the lives of sharecroppers. I know that I ought to be ashamed for having no ambition." The eggshell cup of chocolate began to tremble.

"Patrick?" Samuel's husky voice went soothing. "No one needs to be ashamed of nothin'. We are who we are."

"I could stay with Remy and want nothing else. I would be whatever he wished of me."

"It's the same for me, honey. I do my work here as they need, and the rest of my work I do for Joseph in our rooms."

"Ah, now, I should come eat here more often, me, if this is what we talkin' on." Jean slumped down in a chair beside him with a happy sigh. "Cake!"

Patrick was surprised Jean could sit at all. Last night Jean had been in the dining room, eating draped over Isaiah's knees.

The man did love to have his bottom reddened. Truth be told, the more Patrick learned about his friends, the more relieved he was. He wasn't alone in his needs. Perhaps they were perversions, but he would not be alone in hell.

"Try the lemon one." Samuel pushed the sweet over. "It's got a bite to it."

"I love lemon." They always had the most decadent treats at the club. Good thing Remy kept him in top condition.

They nibbled the sweets, sharing between them. Jean chattered endlessly at them, and Samuel listened, still and quiet.

Not long after, another young man joined them, one Patrick had not met. He had jet black hair and bright green eyes and a smile that was impossible to resist. "Samuel. Jean. Introduce me?"

His accent had a lilt to it, one that spoke of Ireland, maybe.

"Tyrone Shea, meet Patrick Daniels."

He stood, held one hand out. "Pleased, sir."

"Pleasure to meet you!" Tyrone pumped his hand. "May I join you lads?"

"Sit, Ty. Sit." Jean shoved a chair out with his foot, the noise screeching, horrible.

Patrick jumped, and Samuel glared at Jean. "What you all rude for today, son?"

"I said he could sit, *oui?* He welcome w'it us."

Patrick's head began to ache, the throb dull, but threatening to sharpen.

"Thank you." Tyrone sat, smiling all around. "Cakes. Goodness, I love these violet ones."

Samuel nodded and lifted one finger, ordering another round. The waiter nodded and whisked away empty plates, returning with more chocolate, a teapot and cup for Tyrone, and more cakes and sweets.

"So, lad, who are you? How did you come to be here?"

Patrick blinked, then looked to Samuel. He felt off balance, and he had no idea why.

Samuel only smiled slightly. "Patrick came in with Canaan, Ty. He's still on the mend."

"Ah." The pounding in his head grew sharp for a moment and Ty's eyes landed on him.

Ty's gaze sharpened, and Patrick shook his head, pushing away his plate as nausea swept him.

"Tyrone!" Samuel snapped out the name. "Have a care."

The table clattered and he heard the tinkling of the crystals in the chandelier, the drops clicking together and making tinny music.

"Patrick?" Jean looked from him to the ceiling.

He needed Remy. Needed his lover, his friend. His angel. Patrick squeezed his eyes closed, calling out with his heart. *Remy. Please.*

Samuel took his hand, holding on, which was dear, and possibly dangerous. "Honey, you just need to breathe. Ty, you got a bad habit of poking in tender spots."

Tyrone made a distressed noise. "Shite, lads, I didn't know he was that new."

Another hand landed on his arm, Jean's worried voice poking through. "It's okay, *cher*. All is well."

A plate on the table cracked right down the middle. He needed to think. Of Remy. Just Remy.

"*Bébé.* Did you call me?" Remy's smooth as caramel words

slid over his raw nerves, calming him.

"Yessir." Oh. Oh, his love. "Please. I need you."

"I'm right here." When he opened his eyes, he was standing in a hallway with Remy holding his hands, smiling into his eyes. "I missed the cakes, no?"

"I'm sorry. It hurt. It hurt deep inside."

"In your head?" When he nodded, Remy sighed. "I had no idea Tyrone was staying in, *mon doux*. Sammy and Jean are safe, but Ty… He's a good man, but he's nosy."

"I didn't mean to."

Remy snorted. "You did well. You called for me, you listened to your friends, and you controlled yourself."

"Things broke."

"Nothing flew."

"Right. Not a thing." He smiled faintly. "I'm hard on dishes."

"So? I am proud, *bébé*."

Remy wrapped around him, hugging him gently, rocking him for a moment.

Patrick hung on, breathing, his heart finally slowing. Remy. Yes.

"Shall we return, *bébé*? Or were you done?"

"I—" Patrick took a deep breath and squared his shoulders. "I owe the gents a goodbye, at least, and I never got your book at the library."

"Good man. I could have a coffee, myself."

"The lemon cake is special." He twined his fingers with Remy's when Remy reached for his hand.

The table had been reset when they arrived and Ty stood as they reached him.

"Forgive me, would you? I meant no offense."

"None taken. I just… My head hurts some."

Ty's face crumpled with concern. "I'm so sorry. I didn't know."

He held out one hand. "You do now. I reckon we'll start anew."

Tyrone beamed at him, shaking his hand. "Good man. Good man. Thank you."

"Remy would like coffee, please."

The waiter nodded, and Patrick waited for Remy to sit before sinking down at his lover's feet. He put his head in Remy's lap, knowing no one would look down on him for it.

"He's meant for this life, Remy. Meant to be with you." Samuel's words were self-assured, calm.

"I know, Sammy." Remy stroked his hair. "Who has a pocket watch? I want to see how much time expires before the other masters arrive."

"It will be no time at all, I vow."

Patrick chuckled. No, he supposed not. Waves of agitation seemed to bring other members of the club running. His pain was gone, Remy's fingers gentle and sure.

Tyrone chuckled. "Sadly, I am between Masters at the moment." With his eyes closed, Patrick heard the distress behind the laugh.

"Someone will come for you, *cher*. Someone right. Someone that understands."

"I hope so, Remy."

"They will."

Patrick opened his eyes just enough to watch Joseph, who strode up to take the chair next to Samuel. Sammy. That suited him. Samuel's chin was tilted, the kiss Joseph gave Sammy fiery, threatening to set the room aflame.

God in heaven, he loved that. That these men had such an intense, wondrous connection. That he and Remy were not the only ones who loved deeply.

For the first time in his life, Patrick felt as if he could be settled, as if he were home.

He kissed Remy's fingers when they grazed his lips. This was his place. Now he had to simply fight to keep it.

Chapter Twenty

Julian stopped Remy on his way out of the main common room of the club. He'd run out to pick up Patrick's new clothes from the tailor, something he thought important before he took Patrick out on the town for the first time.

"Ah, Remy. Just the man I was looking for. May I have a word?"

"Of course. I've been to get proper attire for my boy. He's progressing beautifully, wouldn't you say?" He refused to allow his nerves to show.

"I would. In fact, I had supper with Matthias last night in order to discuss him. Your boy. Come sit with me."

He handed off the packets of clothing to an attendant along with instructions for his boy to draw them a bath, then he went to sit and hear what the owners had decided.

Julian waited for him to sit, then settled across from him. Those silvery eyes caught his, and Julian smiled. "Matt still has his doubts, but Koni agrees with me. Your boy is ready to go home with you."

"Yes. Yes, he's expressed his desire to see my home. He has made friends here, but…" Samuel had been quite clear that his Paddy was a bit of a beacon.

"Precisely. You two are welcome any time, and you know it. However, the wing you're staying in has grown three full halls of new rooms." One silver gilt brow waggled. "The house is tempted by him, and familiarity will cause it to use him."

"We don't want that." Remy trod carefully, not sure what

exactly Julian wanted. "Shall we go today?"

"You can go tomorrow. Ease him into it and let the boys send him off." Jules' smile called to his gator spirit. "Give the club something to remember."

"That I can do. Thank you, Julian. It means a lot that you trust me to do this."

"There is no one that can care for him more than you."

"No one," he agreed. "I'll make the arrangements."

"If there's anything you need, as always, you have our support." Julian's tone told Remy it was time to go.

"*Merci.*" He rose, his mind racing with plans.

He hurried to their rooms, opening the door to the vision of Patrick's bare ass bent over the tub. Even as agitated as he was, Remy paused to admire, closing the door behind him and turning the latch.

Patrick stood, smiling for him. "Remy. The water is ready."

"I see that, *bébé*. They brought the clothes?"

"They did. They're laid out on the bed. You spoil me." Patrick took a step closer to him. "What's wrong?"

"Nothing is wrong, *lapin*. I'm just very excited." It was true. Patrick needed to see his home. To be in his bed.

"Oh? What's happening?"

Remy went to his lover and took Patrick's hands in his. "Tomorrow we get to go home to my house."

Patrick searched his eyes. "Your home? Permanently?"

"*Oui, bébé.* Home with me."

His lover nodded, a slow smile blooming over the chiseled face. "I never thought you'd ask."

"Tomorrow morning." Remy tugged Patrick close for a kiss. "I'll send word to my staff."

Patrick's lips clung to him, the connection soft, steady.

Remy felt as if he were standing at the edge of Lake Pontchartrain, ready to swim across on nothing but faith alone.

He cupped Patrick's bare ass, rubbing him against his clothes. The rasp of fabric had to itch, had to be maddening.

Patrick shuddered, hands on his shoulders. "More."

"Needy *garçon*," he teased. Patrick was becoming quite the wanton, ready to love him at anytime and anyplace. Remy wanted him right back, and he reached out, cupping Patrick's stiffening package.

"Yes. I need. What do you want me to do, Remy? Tell me?"

"Mmm. Over the bed, *bébé*. Spread wide for me and give yourself over."

"Yes, sir." Patrick turned immediately, bending over the bed mattress and spreading his legs wide. His ass and balls lay open to Remy's view.

Remy hummed softly, admiring the dull flush that began to climb the muscled thighs. He flexed his hands, not sure where to start.

"Will you hold yourself open for me?" he asked, smiling as the bedstead trembled. "Focus, *bébé*."

"Sorry." The breathless laugh made Remy smile. Patrick propped up his chest on a pillow before reaching back to spread his cheeks. No shame, just an eager obedience. The tiny hole waited for his attention, but he waited, letting the moment stretch, testing his *bébé*'s control.

Patrick's arms shook, his leg muscles flexing, but nothing in the room moved otherwise.

"*Bon*." He leaned down and licked a long, gentle line along Patrick's crease.

Patrick went up on tiptoe, his hips swaying. "Remy?"

"Mmmhmm?"

"Remy, you cannot…"

"Oh, *bébé*. There is nothing I cannot, love."

"We should bathe before the water gets cold."

"Would that make you feel better?" Oh, he could see the

benefits of washing Patrick inside and out, making his lover squirm.

Patrick nodded. "You...I...Yes. Yes, please."

"Sweet innocent. Come with me." Remy led Patrick to the tub. "Stand up in the tub, *mon doux*. Then bend and grasp the sides so you're presented like you were at the bed."

The look he got was wide-eyed, part panicked horse, part pure desire, but his lover did as Remy requested. He needed his hands so he didn't slip, but Remy could spread those cheeks easily on his own. Now to find the softest bathing cloth.

He made sure to touch constantly, pinching and stroking Patrick's ass, the crease where leg met hip.

Patrick was swaying, dancing, his balls swinging. Beauty. He wet the cloth, the water dripping down against Patrick's ass, sliding down to dampen the sweet hole.

Shivering, Patrick moaned his name, a sound he heard in his dreams. *Dieu*, he loved this one so.

"I will touch you everywhere, *bébé*. You are mine. My own."

"Yes. Everywhere." The water lapped at the sides of the tub, but only because Patrick shifted his weight from foot to foot.

"Everywhere." He touched the cloth to Patrick's crease and his boy stood, ass clenching. Had anyone ever been so perfectly innocent? He slapped one ass cheek with his other hand. "Back into position."

"I—"

"Now, *bébé*." Another swat and Patrick bent back down, chest working like a bellows.

He dipped the cloth in the water, then dribbled more, watching Patrick tremble. "You're perfect, *bébé*. Did you know?" Remy tapped that entrance with the cloth.

"You make me ache."

"I hope I always do." He would make it his best work, in fact. Remy knew his place in life now, and he would keep Patrick safe, keep him happy as long as he lived.

"I do too."

The simple words warmed him and he rubbed that tiny hole with the cloth, pressing in with one finger. He would clean Patrick well, even though his *bébé* tasted like heaven without the bath. Then he would drive Patrick mad.

With every touch, Patrick shivered, and the low moans filled the air. Such amazing surrender. His Patrick was so sensitive, tender and made for his attention.

Remy leaned down and bit one taut ass cheek, his inner gator eager to leave a mark.

"Remy!"

"Call me sir, *bébé*." He craved that, loved to hear it.

He bit again, and the wild cry, the "sir" rang out and filled the air.

Remy pushed two fingers inside Patrick's ass, washing thoroughly. He licked and nibbled at the butt cheek nearest him, tasting water and skin. His beloved began rocking back, taking him, a needy song on the air.

He gave more, pushing Patrick to hold himself up and not slip. Remy wanted to put his whole hand inside his boy as he had seen Joseph do to Sammy once, but that could wait. Tonight he would use his mouth.

If his *bébé* kept his control, then he would consider it a success. He knew the pleasure of having a man lick and lave the most private part of you.

The idea made his ass clench. He chuckled, pushing and pulling, letting Patrick feel every touch deeply. Remy curled his fingers, stroking when he found spots that made his *bébé* grunt and wag his hips.

He stayed with that for a moment, working relentlessly. Patrick cried out again, and he thought it was time. He pulled free, then rinsed Patrick thoroughly.

"Back to the bed," Remy said, slapping that ass.

Patrick grunted in response, then spun around and kissed him so fiercely that his breath caught in his chest.

Remy laughed when they broke for air, his joy impossible to contain. "Are you disobeying me, *lapin*?"

"You never said nothing about not kissing."

"Oh ho! Cheater." He kissed Patrick again. "To the bed, *bébé*. Bend and spread and present yourself."

He could watch the flush on his *bébé*'s cheeks for an eternity and he hoped the familiar eagerness never faded. Patrick whirled and marched to the bed, then bent, propped, and spread himself once more.

Remy nodded approvingly before kneeling behind Patrick. "Ready, *mon doux*?"

"Yes. Yes, sir. God, I have need of you."

"I want to taste you." He pushed at Patrick's hands, spreading those cheeks wider, the little hole totally exposed. He blew air across it, sensitizing it. If Patrick's fingers dug in any harder, he'd leave bruises on the fine skin.

Remy licked his lips before leaning close, brushing his lips against Patrick's most sensitive skin.

"Oh, sweet Heavens."

Oh, this was altogether more earthly. He licked at Patrick's hole, humming, loving it. The scent of his lover — clean and male, musky and perfect — surrounded him. He pressed his tongue against Patrick's flesh, listening to Patrick moan.

The bath, the bed, the chandelier — not a thing moved. Not a bit.

Pride swelled in his chest. Focus was becoming Patrick's strong suit.

He lapped gently, tracing a lazy circle around Patrick's wrinkled hole. He wanted to build slowly, let Patrick feel every level of sensation. He stroked the line of puckered skin above

Patrick's hanging sac, teasing him mercilessly.

Patrick rocked, back and forth rather than front to back, wagging almost.

Randomly he would back away, offer the stinging sensation of a bite on the back of Patrick's thigh, on one ass cheek, on one finger. Patrick's grip tightened, knuckles white, but nothing crashed or splashed, even though he hadn't emptied the tub yet.

"Good. So good, *bébé*. You are doing so well."

"Thank you. Thank you, sir."

"I love that. Have I said?" He knew he had, but he needed to offer praise.

"You have. Samuel looks so at peace when he calls Joseph sir."

"It makes him happy." He fingered that sweet ass while he talked, wanting to make Patrick fly.

"Yes. More, please."

"More," Remy agreed, bending to his task once more. He would shock his *bébé* with a deep tongue push.

The tiny ring of muscles gripped his tongue, Patrick gasping loudly. That skin was so hot, and Remy stroked Patrick's thighs with his hands, licking and pushing with his tongue. His lover danced beneath him, wild gasps on the air. They moved together, Patrick pushing back, him working that tiny hole.

He reached between Patrick's legs and grabbed the heavy cock that waited for him, swinging and leaking precious drops of need. He gathered up the moisture on his fingers so he could taste that as well. Salty and rich, Patrick made his eyes cross.

Swaying, Patrick babbled nonsense words, so heated now that if they were in the bath the water would steam.

Finally he pulled back, slicking his cock with a trembling hand and jacking himself with firm, sure tugs.

"Please. Please, Remy. Sir. Master."

"Yes." Remy stood, pushing his prick against that needy

entrance. His Patrick pushed back with a wild cry, swallowing his cock with the single thrust. He rewarded that with a deep bite to Patrick's shoulder, knowing the sting would madden his lover.

Patrick began to thrust, slamming back against him, wild, and he grabbed his *bébé*'s hips, wrenching control back. He dug in his fingers into those muscles, applying pressure.

"My rules, *bébé*. Mine."

"I know. I can't... I need."

"So beautifully, too. Still, my choice." Remy slapped one thigh, smiling when Patrick moaned. Then he began thrusting again. He chose a fast pace, at least until Patrick began slamming back, then he slowed. Every time Patrick tried to wrest control from him, he stilled, waiting. Nothing broke or fell to the floor.

So proud. He was so damn proud of his lover. Remy pushed in deeper, rocking his hips, rolling Patrick farther onto the mattress. He whispered words, endearments, sex words. He wanted Patrick mad for him. He could feel Patrick's body fluttering around his prick, nearly milking him. The action made Remy grit his teeth to hold on, then reach down around Patrick's hip to touch Patrick's cock.

"Remy! Remy, please." Not silent, his *bébé*. Not silent at all.

"Soon, *bébé*. Focus on me. Listen to my body so we go together." Remy swore he could feel it like a splash of river water when Patrick's mind landed its weight on him. His balls drew up, and he hung on by a thread. He refused to spend until his *bébé* did, until Patrick emptied himself.

Patrick took everything he gave, skin flushed, muscles straining. "May I touch myself, sir?"

"*Oui, bébé. Oui.* I want to feel your touch all around me."

Patrick nodded, propping up on one hand and using the other to stroke his cock. As soon as Patrick touched himself, Remy felt those inner muscles clamp down on him, squeezing.

"Yes." He bit the world out and began to slam in, over and

over, again and again. He was close, so close he could barely breathe, and that was when Patrick went over. He felt it as surely as he felt that tight channel slam closed around him, pulling Remy's little death out of him as well.

He filled his boy, moaning as he slumped over Patrick's back.

Patrick held them up, panting, until Remy could roll to one side.

Tomorrow he would be in his own bed, and Patrick with him. He smiled wide, the pleasure in that idea immense. Yes. Tonight they would give Patrick dinner with his new friends. Tomorrow? Was only for them.

"We're really going to go, then? You'll show me your home?"

"We are. Oh, *bébé*, I cannot wait." He wanted to show Paddy all the wonderful things he'd found, all of the rooms in his strange little house.

"I confess that I'm eager to see a place that is yours and yours alone."

"It feels as if I've been traveling," Remy mused. "I'm ready, as well."

"I'm glad you found me. That I was given to you?"

"No, I volunteered to care for you, *lapin*. I just happened to be here when Canaan brought you."

Patrick nodded, lips brushing his. "I'm glad."

"So am I, *bébé*. So am I." He was in love, in fact. "Your *amis* wish to send you off tonight."

"Will I see them again, once I leave?"

"Oh, yes. I intend for us to come often to the club."

"Good. Samuel's a fine man and so is Jean."

"They are good boys, and you can learn a great deal from them. Shall we have that bath, *bébé*?"

"I think we ought, yes."

"Then you can dress me for dinner. I'll send Daniel to see if you should dress or not." He waited to see how Patrick would react to that.

The look he received was pure confusion. "I don't understand."

"Well, it depends on what sort of party your friends are planning." He watched Patrick closely. "They may decide all Sirs get a naked boy."

"You cannot be serious." Patrick stared at him, then headed for the tub. "Naked. At supper."

"Mmm." He rang for Daniel. Yes, he should definitely ask about attire.

Patrick sank into the water as Daniel appeared.

"Sir?"

"I need to send a message to Isaiah and Joseph, please. Inquire about the clothing, *oui*? For supper."

"Yes, sir. Of course. There will be a soirée in the ballroom?"

"I hope so." He chuckled when Daniel left them, moving to join Patrick in the tub.

"A soirée, huh? You know we just have hoedowns back home? Church socials?"

"We had grand balls in my old home. My *maman*, she loved to dance."

"Do you?" Patrick began to wash him.

"I do. I would rather dance with you than with some *demoiselle* in a gown, but I enjoy it." He hadn't danced in years. Once, in San Francisco, there had been a huge redheaded miner who had waltzed like a dream, and had swept Remy around the floor as if he were the *demoiselle*...

"I can waltz." Patrick never ceased to surprise him.

"Can you? We must find some music." He kissed Patrick's mouth, amazed at the contentment he could feel in Patrick's heart.

They held one another until Daniel appeared beside the tub. "The Masters say that formal attire is unnecessary."

"And for my boy?"

"That is, of course, your discretion."

"Thank you, Daniel."

Daniel faded like the ghost he was, and Patrick shook his head. "That's unnerving sometimes."

"Yes, and I have seen it many times."

"So, am I to be naked for supper?" Patrick's bravado didn't fool him.

He pondered that. There was a delicious and literal stripping down with such an act, but again, he was unsure whether he wished to share Patrick's body, even the sight of it. Perhaps when they had been together longer…

No, tonight he would let Patrick dress for dinner.

At least partially.

"Your trousers will be sufficient, *bébé*. I wish to play with those sweet nips during our meal." A fine compromise, if he did say so himself. The lads could admire, but Remy would know what lay hidden.

Patrick groaned, nipples drawing up tight, as if begging his immediate attention.

Remy laughed. "See? You're already showing off proud."

"Remy!"

Oh, this was delicious entertainment. He reached out to tweak those nipples. "What? How can this be worse than going with a plug inside you?"

"No one knew."

"Nonsense." Samuel and Jean, Isaiah and Joseph: these were experienced men. Patrick walked like a dream when he was filled and plugged.

"Well, no one saw." Patrick's cheeks might catch fire.

"They will see your sweet buds, the way they will be pink and swollen, *bébé*."

"Oh." Patrick stared into his eyes. "Will that please you?"

"It will. You will be excited, you will prove your control, and

I will be able to touch as I will. It will be bliss."

"Then we should get dressed." Patrick's happy smile put joy in Remy's heart.

"After we soak a moment more, hmm? I am enjoying you."

"I love you," Patrick said, simple and clear.

"As I love you, *bébé*."

"Let's float." Patrick pulled him into those strong arms, the water still warm and pleasant. Remy let himself be held, his lips against Patrick's neck. Patrick touched him, stroked him and caressed him like he was precious.

He hummed, loving the simple touches, the closeness.

"I can't wait to see your home."

"*Oui, bébé*. I am so excited." He was, more and more every moment. He'd been worried when Julian had pulled him aside, but now he knew all would be well.

He was going to take Patrick home and keep him, forever.

Chapter Twenty One

The busy streets, the noise and dust and smoke… Well, they all conspired to leave Patrick teetering on his very last nerve by the time they reached Remy's home.

The little house was tall and narrow, tucked in between two similar homes. Row houses, Remy called them. Remy's was neoclassical in style and build of brick. The big bay window in the front invited him to peek inside, but then Remy took his hand.

"Come in, *bébé*."

"Is it always this loud, Remy?"

"Oh, *mon doux*, this is not such a busy time." Remy smiled, those dark eyes full of sympathy. "Come inside. You will find it a comfort."

The door opened and he walked in, the world closing out behind them.

The foyer was, thankfully, dark and cool. A table sat in the center of the little round area, a huge spray of flowers sitting in a blue and white vase. It was so very normal, so lovely. Unexpected.

To one side lay a parlor full of wonders. To the other were a hall and the stairs leading up.

He wasn't sure which way to look, which way to go. "This is yours. It smells like you."

"Does it?" Remy seemed delighted by that idea. "Come see. I have a clock here that was *maman*'s. She sent it to me on the train when I bought this house."

Remy drew him to the parlor, to a carved mantle with a gorgeous clock sitting in the pride of place. The thing was a Baroque beauty, but what caught him was the wild array of colors and styles. An Egyptian chaise. A classical bust of some Caesar. A huge chair that seemed almost medieval.

It felt like...hell, he didn't know. Like the museums that he'd read about in Momma's books, he guessed. There were just enough knick knacks strewn around to flavor the room with exotic spice, but not so many he worried he would break something.

"The spice chest is from the West Indies." Remy trailed his fingers over a carved chest sitting on a stand.

He didn't even know where that was, but he thought the work was amazing — he'd seen his pappy carve toys and bird calls, all sorts of things, but nothing so intricate.

"Now the dining room, hmm?" Remy held out one hand to him.

"Everywhere, Remy. I want to know it all." His curiosity burned him.

Remy laughed like a happy boy and pulled him along at a trot. Oh, gracious. The dining room looked as if it belonged to a sultan out of an old storybook. He stared, open-mouthed. Somehow the room screamed decadence and sensuality, and yet it was simply a dining room.

"Sometimes I eat on pillows on the floor," Remy murmured.

"It suits you, like a storybook pasha."

Remy clapped his hands. "Just so. I learned it from a very exotic man out West."

Patrick wasn't sure whether to be pleased or jealous. "I hope you won't find me to be a bore."

"Never. You're mine." Remy led him to the kitchen. "Are you hungry? I had cook leave us nibbles. I want to introduce you to everyone at once, later."

"Are they…are they like Daniel here?"

"No, *bébé*. They're all alive."

He flushed, but the question had begged asking.

The kitchen was clean, cozy, obviously loved and well-cared for, with a heavy aura of spice hanging in the air. He breathed deep, smelling some sort of bread.

"Come, have a bite. There's spiced oil to dip and some cheese."

The spread was as fine as any Momma's cook had put up. The cheese was delicate, flaky, making his lip purse with pleasure.

"Mmm. You like that, do you?"

"I do! Sour and salty, but so good."

"Feed me a bite?"

The temptation to tease and ask Remy if he was broken was huge, but he refrained, still too unnerved to play. This was Remy's place, his territory. Patrick picked up a bite and offered it to Remy's lips.

"Mmm. It is luscious, isn't it?"

He nodded and dared to lean forward, lick once at Remy's mouth. "Definitely."

Remy flushed, dark eyes glittering. "Soon I will show you the bedroom, *bébé*."

"I am eager to see it."

"I'm eager to see you spread on our bed."

Our bed. The words vibrated inside him. He didn't know… Patrick worried that Remy felt responsible for him. That this was a job. Then Remy said things like that and it erased his worry, eased his mind.

He took Remy's hand again, then grabbed a plate of goodies with his other hand. "Show me."

Remy made the best sounds for him, raw and wild and happy. They ran up the stairs together, their steps pounding and creaking. One long hall led back from the landing on the second floor, and they passed several doors before Remy led him to the master suite.

It was a huge room, but simple, with huge dark furniture and a vast fireplace with an overstuffed chair and an ottoman before the hearth.

A small, white and black tiled bathroom occupied one corner, clearly built in later than the house was crafted.

"A bath inside, in your own room." He was impressed.

"I put it in when I saw the rooms in Club Raven." Remy laughed. "I felt decadent."

"It's fancy." He moved to the bedstead, hand wrapping around one thick post. "This is fine."

"I had a vision. A year ago. There was a man, a big one. Tall. Broad." Remy stared at him. "Blond."

His body began to flush, his cock going heavy behind his buttons. "Yes?"

"Strong. One who needed a heavy bedstead to hold him." Remy stroked the bedpost opposite the one he held, hand rubbing up and down.

"Hold him?" His eyes were fastened on Remy's hand, the rhythm of the motions.

"Mmm. When I tie him to it. He's *fort*. He can pull and bend things. The bed needs to hold." Remy worked his hand faster. "I may need to spread him wide, let him watch over me as I sleep while he is hard and bound."

He swallowed hard. "Oh. I— God."

"No, *bébé*." Remy sat on the edge of the bed. "This is a matter of men."

Remy's hand cupped his crotch, rolled him, pushing and proving his need.

Patrick went up on tiptoes, Remy's very touch always sending him to heaven. He wanted that hand on his skin, not on his stiff new trousers.

"There are many secret places, you know? High and low, midway. Spots to bind you and spread you."

"High? How? Wouldn't it hurt to be bound up above you?"

"Your hands at the top, your feet at the bottom, your cock hard and needy where it cannot be touched."

"Like a statue?" His cock was going to bust out of his pants.

"An erotic one." Remy petted him, pushed at him. "Like the paintings at the club."

Those portraits. Oh, dear God. The idea alone made him sweat. He was curious about some of them. Intensely.

"I can smell you, *bébé*."

"I just bathed."

"Your arousal is like the finest perfume."

The things that Remy said made him dizzy with need, made him arch into Remy's hand like a cat in heat. Patrick spread his legs and pushed, hoping Remy might punish him for taking control.

"Look at you, wanton." Remy's words made him groan.

Patrick nodded. "I need. I'll always tell you when I do."

"Strip down for me, *bébé*. I think you need a sleeve for that needy cock, something to help control your desire."

"I do." He stripped out of the new clothes hurriedly, because he was unused to so much cloth now. It itched.

"I will keep you bare as the day you were born, *bébé*." Remy opened a drawer in the chest, pulling out pieces of leather — straps and cuffs.

"Are these all yours?"

"I had them made for you. I sent them over last night by courier."

"Made for me?"

"Yes, *mon doux*. I wanted something made to my specifications, just for you."

Remy nodded, motioning him closer. As he stood there,

Remy wrapped his cock and balls with thin strips of leather, braiding it around his prick.

Patrick stared down, his mind trying to process what he was seeing.

"Lovely. One day I will embed a ring right here." Remy tapped the slit of his cock. "And loop the leather through it."

"Oh." His lips opened on the sound, his balls pulling up. He wasn't sure if it was fear or desire that made them.

He was equally sure it didn't matter to Remy a bit which one it was.

"*Oui, bébé.* I will put rings in these, too." Remy reached up to pinch his nipples.

He shook his head, but he knew he would do it, just because Remy asked. In fact, he was desperate to see what it felt like, what Remy would do with such rings.

"*Oui.* You want to know, don't you? You crave it."

"I do. Anything that pleases you."

"Mmm. I will have Allan teach me to do it. I don't want anyone else touching you that way."

A drop of clear need formed at the tip of his cock. He stared at it, watched as Remy scooped it up with one finger before tasting it.

"Mmm. Delicious."

"Sir." He shook a little, the stress of the day threatening to overwhelm him.

"Look at me, Paddy."

He met those amazing, warm dark eyes. "Yes, sir."

"Focus on me. I want you. *Je t'adore.* You are safe here."

"Your home."

"Ours. Our home." Remy took him by the hand and pulled him into the bed.

Oh, he could feel why Remy had been so eager to be home. He'd never felt a mattress so soft. Clouds. It was like clouds, but it held them up firmly, as well.

"Yes, you see! The things we can do, no?"

"Yes. No. Please." He felt dizzy.

Remy pressed him down on the bed. "Yes. Such pleasurable games."

"Yes." He unfastened the tie that held back Remy's ebony hair.

Remy laughed, then bent to kiss him, their connection burning him to the ground. He hadn't been forbidden to touch, so Patrick sank his hands into Remy's hair, the heavy strands curling around his fingers.

His.

The thought made him moan. His own beloved.

Remy nodded, kissing him again as if to say *yes, yes I am.*

He found himself surrounded by Remy's scent, by Remy's need. The bed cradled him almost like another lover and, when Remy crawled atop him, padded straps in hand, Patrick raised his arms to grip the bedposts.

"My obedient *bébé.*" The praise rained down on him like the late summer storm battering against the windows.

"I try, sir. I do." He smiled, loving the way Remy shook when he said *sir.*

He loved the kisses even more, loved how they burned him to the ground. Remy finally pulled back to breathe, and that was when Patrick was tied to the bedstead.

"My *bébé.* My love. I will keep you forever, I vow."

"Be careful what you promise, Remy. I would stay with you for an eternity."

"Then we'll make it so." Remy stroked his arms so lightly it tickled.

He twisted and tugged at the cuffs, but they held. "Did you think you would have someone to bring home, when you agreed to care for me?"

"Oh, *bébé*, I would have stayed forever at Raven for you, like Joseph and his Samuel. I had hoped, though."

"They think I'm safer here."

"I do, too." Remy slid one hand down the middle of Patrick's body. He loved the sight of that dark hand on his skin, the pressure of Remy's touch. Remy tugged at the hairs low on his belly before stroking through the curls at the base of his cock. "Golden crown here."

He still wasn't sure how to respond to those wicked, warm words.

Remy's warm, rich chuckle slid over his raw nerves. "You're still so innocent sometimes."

"I've never met anyone who says the things you do."

"I know, *mon doux*. I know. I surprise myself sometimes, but I want you so." Remy was all but dancing for him, undulating against him. "I have need of you, *bébé*."

"I'm yours. Yours, Remy."

"I know." Remy threw off shirt and trousers, struggling not to overbalance. Patrick drew his knees up, cradling Remy, offering support.

"Thank you, *lapin*." Remy kissed him again, stroking his skin, fingers digging in under his arms, tugging the hairs he found there and making him gasp and twist. No one had touched him there, not like this, and it shocked him, how his nerves jumped. "Sensitive!"

Remy seemed amused, aroused. "Amazing, no? No one thinks of these places." Those clever fingers found the crease between his thigh and hip.

Every one of those touches sent light through him and he pushed that into Remy, knowing that Remy could hold it, take it in. Remy seemed to take whatever he gave and use it, glowing from inside. Remy nodded for him, stroked the insides of his thighs.

He shivered, his nipples pulling into hard points, his cock bouncing when Remy slapped it lightly. It couldn't go far in its binding, but it could ache so well…

"Mmm. I think that suits you, a whisper of pain."

"I don't— I think you suit me." That way he didn't have to admit he liked the sting.

"I know I suit you, *bébé*. I was made for you."

"You think so?" He wanted to believe that so badly. He didn't want to be a burden.

"I know it. I need you more than my next breath." Remy scooted up in his lap, cock rubbing Patrick's bound prick. Oh. Oh, that was maddening. He couldn't feel like he was used to, like he expected. The separation made things so— Oh, he didn't know. It made him crazy.

Remy chuckled softly, laughing at him, at his need. There seemed no cruelty in it, only joy.

"Evil man," he whispered.

"Am I?" Remy tilted his head. "I suppose so." Remy flicked the tip of his cock with strong fingers.

He gasped, his eyes rolling and teeth clicking together. He had no idea what to do; his hands and cock were bound, and all he could do was take what Remy gave him.

"You are mine, *bébé* — all of you, cock, body, soul."

"Everything." He bucked up when Remy slipped a fingertip into his slit, left bare by the bindings.

"Mmhmm." Remy pushed a little deeper, a little harder.

"Oh!" His ass clenched, his balls pulling up tight, and Remy's smile was pure evil. "Remy. You. The way you touch me. I never could have imagined you."

"And yet now you have me." Remy swooped down, licked the tip of his cock.

"Sir!" He focused on Remy, on the sweet, wet heat.

"Yes." God help him, Remy sounded so satisfied. That

mouth worked him, lips and tongue driving him mad.

He babbled, tugging at the cuffs, his entire body shaking with pleasure. His cock felt constricted, but he also felt safe knowing he couldn't release unless Remy let him. It was deliciously comforting, suiting him to the bone.

Remy was the perfect Sir. The best lover. And Patrick belonged here.

"You do belong here, *bébé*. With me. I'll not let you go."

"Did you hear me? Did I speak?"

"What?" Remy's dark eyes narrowed.

"I didn't speak." He was fairly sure.

"What do you mean, *bébé*?" Remy looked confused, lips pursed.

"I'm sure it was nothing."

"Mmm." Remy nuzzled his cock before pushing up once more to smile into his eyes. He smiled back, refusing to worry on things any longer than he must. Remy was too warm and giving, too devious with that look in his eye. "I do like having you in my bed."

"I know." He laughed and tugged his arms. "It does hold well, too."

"Yes. I have desired someone to keep and need, to be my own for a lifetime." Remy licked his lower lip. "I dreamed about you."

Pretty words.

"Did you? I didn't know to dream of you, of this, but I... You know I was caught...He was a boy like me and I wanted him."

"Tell me about him? Does it hurt to think about him?" Remy didn't seem jealous.

"The whipping I got from my father hurt, the shame when Henry found out was worse. He was a hand at the farm. My father cut him...removed his manhood. I was lucky."

"Oh, *bébé*." Remy immediately pressed against his chest, kissing and loving him.

This kiss was soft, sweet, a true comfort, leaving him feeling like he was wrapped in pure bliss. He could forget about all his former troubles when Remy touched him so.

He stretched long, his back popping with the motion. Remy smiled at him, one hand cupping the back of his head, fingers coming dangerously close to that…that spot. That…

"Don't."

"Why?"

"My brother—"

Remy shook his head. "No, *bébé*. This is about you. Not him."

"He died." That was the most important thing. Wasn't it?

"*Non.*" Remy's word was like a shot. Like the shot Patrick had taken in battle. "The most important thing is that you lived. He is gone. You go on."

"You can hear me." He didn't want to think too much on Henry and how he'd bled out, life coating his chest, his face, wet and thick and sour.

"What?" Remy said it just as he had before, dark brows drawing together.

"You hear my thoughts. You heard me." Patrick knew it. He hadn't spoken.

Remy shook his head. "I'm no mind reader, *bébé*. Perhaps in the Club, where the magic is like a cloak…"

"You heard me." *You can. You hear me. I will not share your secret, Remy.*

Remy blinked. "Patrick. The cards, they speak to me. I know things sometimes. Before they happen. But I don't hear thoughts."

You hear me. A dull anger hit him and he frowned. *I know you can.*

"No." Remy slid off him, pacing the floor beside the bed.

"Are you calling me a liar, lover?" One of the straps around his wrists snapped and he sat up, unfastening the other with quick motions. He would not be thought dishonest.

"No. No, of course not. I'm not talented that way. I'm simple, *bébé*. Not like you."

But you can hear me, he thought, sending it to his lover, much like he offered Remy his will, his body.

Remy whirled to face him, clapping his hands over his ears. "How?"

"Like I would know, lover. Is it so awful? My voice?" What a terrible thought, that Remy had taken so much of him, but would find his thoughts distasteful.

"*Quoi?* No! No, you're the most beautiful thing in the world to me." Remy came to him and took his hands. "What if I begin to hear others? That can drive a man mad."

Patrick shrugged. What did he know of that? "You said you were made for me."

"I am." Remy chuckled. "I am yours as you are mine, *bébé*."

"Then why would you hear anyone else?"

Remy squeezed his hands. "I have no idea."

"No one else hears me." He kissed Remy's cheek. He needed Remy. He'd only just discovered the wonders they could share.

"I want to hear you, *mon doux*. Just not everyone else."

He nodded, kissed Remy's cheek, the corner of his mouth. Remy had taken everything he'd poured in. Remy could do this.

"What do I do?" This was Remy asking him for help for the very first time, and Patrick gave it all the serious thought it deserved.

"I think you should send for your best friends from the club. You don't have to go out that way and you can see if you can hear them." He dared to tease, just a bit. "You don't have a soft spot in your head, do you?"

"Not that I know of." Remy chuckled.

"Do you trust me, Remy?" He asked the question Remy had asked him so many times.

"With my soul."

"Then believe in us. I would not allow you to lose your mind. I need you. You brought me back. I would do it for you."

Remy stopped, stilling completely. Then he nodded slowly. "I trust you, *bébé*. I do. We'll ask our friends over for supper. Tomorrow. Today is for us. In our home."

Our home. Oh, he did like those words, very much.

Patrick tugged Remy back to the bed. "I think you might need to get the cuff repaired."

"I may have to tan your hide for snapping it." Remy looked altogether too amused by that thought.

"It was your fault." Patrick teased right back, pushing his sir.

"Mine?" The way those eyebrows lifted promised trouble.

His cock began to grow once more, filling the sleeve. "You panicked."

"I never panic."

"You did. I was going to rescue you."

"You did." Remy slid up along his body to kiss him until his ears rang. "You saved me from a very boring life all alone, *bébé*."

He held on, fingers curled in Remy's hair.

Remy could hear him, and, now that Patrick knew it, he was going to take advantage of it. *You make me want wicked things, sir. Perverse things. Things that I never imagined before you.*

Remy started, but then he laughed. "No? You were ready. You just needed me to teach you. I'm honored that I was the one."

He closed his eyes and imagined the pillow whacking Remy's backside, using his arousal and the remainder of his worry to make it work.

"What are you doing, *bébé*?" Remy laughed, the sound delighted. Thrilled.

Hopefully he was playing. Another swack and he had to stop. Doing this on purpose was so much harder than when he had no control.

"Look at you! Are you saying you want a good spanking, *mon doux*? I can give it to you."

"I was playing with you." He wanted Remy's hand, but he wasn't sure whether spanking was the thing. He also wasn't sure if he was ready to ask for it.

Remy tilted his head. "Oh, Patrick. Are you sure? That can be... big."

"Samuel says it is...possible."

Those dark eyes seemed to glow for a moment. "It is. I've never done it, but Joseph and Samuel... demonstrated."

"Remy! You watched?" That was at once scandalous and intensely arousing and the bed might have jumped.

"I did. It was stunning." Remy rose, then patted his belly. "Stay here."

"Where are you going?" He sat up, his hand dropping to his need, stroking it, feeling like the biggest sort of wanton.

"There are things to prepare, *bébé*. I need towels and oil."

"I saw it. On a portrait."

"In the hall on the third floor, no? Oh, those wicked ghosts. I will do it with you, Patrick. I will hold you inside, in my hand."

He couldn't imagine it, but that wasn't quite true, was it? He had imagined it, Remy stretching him, filling him, touching him deeper than anyone ever.

Patrick licked his lips, watching Remy gather supplies. A basin and cloth, towels. A huge bottle of oil.

He gripped his erection tighter, squeezing the leather that bound him, working the tip with his thumb, so that lightning shot up his spine.

"Are you ready for me?" Remy came back to him, lifting his hips to place towels beneath.

"I don't know. I don't know if I can stretch."

"You can. You can take all I give you." Remy spread him wide, then knelt between his legs. "Keep stroking. Imagine when

I place a ring in your tip, when I tie a bow there."

The leather sheath was becoming maddening. Too tight, too scratchy. It threatened to cut off his blood.

"It will keep you in my control, *bébé*."

"I am always, always in your control."

"*Oui*. And I will never hurt you." Remy opened the oil, which had a thick earthy scent,

"This doesn't hurt?" He couldn't believe that.

"If we do this right you will feel full, and there will be times when it borders on too much, but if it hurts, you must tell me." Remy met his gaze. "Immediately."

"I will." But Remy would know.

"Yes." That got him another smile. Remy propped him up on the pillows he'd hit Remy with. "I trust you will come to me, should your talent begin to make itself known."

"I will." They had to trust that he had control. Had to.

"Good. Keep touching, *bébé*."

"Myself?" He rubbed his cock up and down.

"Yes."

It was more than a little maddening, the non-contact, the pressure without sensation. The sleeve kept him from really being able to get a grip, to get friction.

The oil was cold enough to make Patrick jump, but warmed quickly as Remy rubbed it into his hole.

"Such a lovely, tight little hole."

"Remy!" The things his lover said. Out loud. In front of people on occasion. They still scandalized Patrick.

"It's true. We need to loosen you up today, just for this. You'll feel it for days after." Two oily fingers slid deep inside him.

"For days? Samuel said as much." And the man had looked blissful.

"Did he? Such a smart man." Remy worked him open, slowly and carefully, so gently he wanted to scream to go faster. Deeper.

"I want more, Remy. Sir. Please."

"Good *bébé*. Let me know what you need." Remy sank another finger into him, letting him feel the stretch.

"You." And it was simple as that, wasn't it? He needed Remy.

"I love that." Remy found his gaze once more. "I love you."

"I am glad. This would be hard, without love."

"It would. You never have to worry about being anything less than the other half of me." More oil eased the way.

He bent one knee, spread himself wider so that Remy's fingers had more room. That seemed to help, his muscles working, opening up after a moment of tension. Remy moved slowly, three fingers becoming four, that pressure relentless.

"Breathe, Patrick. Remember what I tell you. Focus and breathe."

He nodded, swallowing hard. Focus. Focus and breathe.

As soon as he managed to get a deep breath in, then out, the four fingers fit. Not easily, but it worked.

"Patrick, *bébé*. You forgot to move your hand, love. Stroke yourself."

"I can hardly feel it." Patrick panted, trying to make his hand move.

"You will."

He didn't understand, but he trusted Remy, utterly. He finally got going, sliding his hand up and down his cock.

Remy pushed, then pulled back. In and out for what seemed forever. Finally, Remy pressed against Patrick's belly with his free hand. "Bear down, then release, love."

He closed his eyes, forcing his body to open, to take what Remy offered, but it was so hard. He breathed, blowing out his breath. That relaxed him enough to allow Remy to fold his thumb into his palm, pushing the whole hand inside. He gasped, his shoulders leaving the mattress and Remy's free hand landed in the center of his chest.

"Easy. Easy, *bébé*. Touch the tip of your cock for me, make it sting."

He immediately pinched the slit of his prick closed, his balls pulling up.

"Just so. *Bon.* Keep going, let it make things bigger."

"Bigger. It can't get bigger."

Remy's chuckle bounced over his skin, and the hand inside him twisted.

His toes curled, his breath wheezing out. "Remy. I can't. I don't know what to do."

"Patrick. *Bébé.* On me. Focus on me."

He blinked down, met those dark eyes. Something in him eased with the exchange of energy, and he nodded, his hole opening up and Remy's hand sliding in until his ring of muscles snapped closed around Remy's wrist.

"Master!" The word ripped from him, a rush of pure energy slammed into him. He turned it back, pouring it into Remy, because he couldn't hold it and he couldn't spend to release his tension.

"Yes!" Remy arched, fingers holding his hip, the other hand deep inside him.

"I—" His breath tore out of him, and Patrick might have screamed; he wasn't sure. The world had tightened down to the pressure within him. He felt feverish, his body too big and too small, his skin too tight.

Remy bent forward, lips wrapping around the tip of his cock, the heat sudden and shocking. That rough tongue pushed against his slit, slapping it a bit.

He sobbed, his body clenching, his thoughts shattering into a million shards. He gave Remy everything that wanted to shake and rattle and break, and Remy gave him love. So much love.

So much need.

His climax rocketed him, went on and on, and he was still

hard at the end. His balls ached, and Remy was moaning, hand moving inside him, just tiny motions that made him feel as if he was losing his mind.

Words hiccupped out of him, but none of them made any sense, not even to him.

I hear you, bébé.

Remy said it in his head. Inside him.

"Yes!" He knew it. He believed it. Patrick gave Remy his joy, his amazement that they were here. Together.

Remy groaned, cock sliding against his leg, leaving needy drops on his skin.

"Please. Please, Remy, I want you to come."

"Soon, *bébé*. Let me ease out."

He didn't want to be empty, but he needed Remy to let his cock loose, wanted them to spend together.

"I'll fill you again, *bébé*, with my seed."

"Yes." He stilled, because he wanted to thrash, wanted to pull back, but he knew that would hurt. Remy petted his belly, murmuring soft praise.

He watched Remy pull back a scant inch at a time, applying more oil as he went. The feeling was indescribable.

"Sir. Sir, you… In me."

"Always, *bébé*. I have held you in the palm of my hand now." Remy grimaced, hand catching when it got to the wrist once more. Oil poured down over his skin, Remy working, twisting the tiniest bit to open him. "Breathe in, very deep. Now out."

He keened as Remy's hand popped out of him, the sudden emptiness overwhelming. His muscles couldn't even clench, he was so open. All he could do was writhe, his bound cock maddening him as Remy disappeared for a moment, leaving him flailing.

Then Remy groaned and suddenly the sweet cock was sliding inside him, driving them together. He could clamp down now, and he knew he wasn't as tight as normal, but it didn't matter. They were joined.

Remy began to work the laces from his cock, baring him, freeing him. Blood rushed to the tip of his prick, his balls pulling up even tighter, and he cried out, arching up.

"So hot, *bébé*! So hot." Remy grabbed his thigh and yanked them tighter together, hips slapping his backside.

Patrick panted, touching Remy's chest, his belly. "Can't hold it. Please."

"Soon. Soon, together. Us."

They rocked so fast, and Patrick felt it in his soul when Remy was ready, when he was about to let go. He grabbed his cock and stroked so they went over the edge together, soaring for what seemed forever.

Heat splashed on his belly and filled him, at the same time. The sensations overwhelmed him, left him shaken and gasping for air. He tried to pet Remy but he had no coordination.

Remy slumped against his chest, gasping.

Slowly they sank together, relaxing deeper and deeper into the mattress.

"*Je t'aime, bébé.* I do."

"Yes. Yes, sir. Thank God for that."

Remy kissed him just before Patrick closed his eyes and fell asleep for the first time in his new home.

It was a fine place to be.

Chapter Twenty Two

The dining room shone in the gaslight, the good crystal a fine counterpoint to the more pedestrian plates. He wasn't using the everyday china for Patrick; he trusted his *bébé* implicitly. No, this was in case Jean had a pout, or Lionel decided to argue with Andrew about something.

He would love to invite Samuel and Joseph, but Sammy never left the club so, instead, he had sent for Isaiah and Jean, and his dear friends Lionel and Andrew. They were not a couple, but they were best friends, and they had talents that would help tell Remy what he wanted to hear.

He needed to know that this talent was specific to his *bébé*, his lover. He needed to know that he wouldn't have to hear anyone else's thoughts.

He hadn't heard the servants, but what if it came on slowly? What if suddenly he was hearing the whole world? Patrick said not, and Remy wanted to believe, but Andrew and Lionel would help.

He trusted Patrick, but what did his lover know about the different talents of their group?

Patrick was laughing in the kitchen, his lover had found friends with his staff, the pirate stories charming him. Remy still kept a horse in the small mews behind his house, as well, and his all around stable master was a gold miner from California who was already terribly fond of his boy.

He looked forward to finding a suitable mount for Patrick and going riding. Maybe he would buy a small property outside of town once Patrick was ready to be out in the world. Somewhere Patrick could have several horses and fewer people to cause his *bébé* to worry.

They could be like the Vanderbilts, having a country home and a city one. Perhaps Samuel would even come to see them then.

"Everything is to your liking, sir?" Germain asked. Germain was his butler and he did a fine job.

"Perfectly. The guests will arrive shortly."

"Yes, sir. Mister Patrick is below stairs with Balou."

"Thank you." He closed his eyes and thought hard. *What are you doing, bébé?*

It took a few moments, then he heard, *Sampling the soup. It's delicious.*

Good. I hear Isaiah's carriage. Isaiah had to have a closed conveyance. Jean could be unpredictable.

Coming. He could hear Patrick searching for his waistcoat. Someone was in the kitchen in his bare shirtsleeves again.

He chuckled, moving one glass, checking the baskets of bread and biscuits.

Soon a warm hand brushed across his ass, stroking him gently. Patrick. His only love.

Remy turned, raising one hand to stroke Patrick's cheek. "You found your jacket."

"Do you approve, sir?" The black frock coat sat well on Patrick's shoulders, the sapphire waistcoat picking up the colors in his *bébé*'s eyes.

"I love it." He brushed imaginary lint off Patrick's arm just as the knocker sounded at the door.

"Come to the parlor, Remy. We must greet your guests."

Yes, it would be unseemly to be caught standing in the dining room, even for a Texan. He chuckled, taking Patrick's hand, and they moved to the parlor together.

Isaiah wore a sober gray suit, and both Andrew and Lionel wore jewel toned waistcoats, under brown or black kit, but Jean… Goodness, he was in pirate regalia.

Patrick almost cheered. "Oh, Jean! You look amazing, like something from a storybook!"

Jean bowed, smiling, his eyes ringed with kohl. "*Merci, mon ami.* I dressed for you."

"You make me wish I had my six shooters and a marshal's badge. We would make a team."

"We would!" Jean came forward to kiss Patrick's cheeks, then his.

Remy chuckled at Jean, so pleased. "Thank you for coming, *mon ami.*"

"I made Isaiah answer right away."

"Have you met Lionel and Andrew, Patrick?" Remy couldn't remember.

Patrick offered a noncommittal smile. "It is good to have your company, y'all."

"Pleasure," Andrew said, stepping up to shake hands. He was a tall, handsome man with blond hair and blue eyes, where Lionel was more slender, with prematurely gray hair and pale eyes.

Patrick shook, confident and sure in his place. It had surprised him, but his *bébé* had been raised in society and simply needed a place, a position at his side.

Lionel came to kiss his cheek, far more intimate than Andrew, before clasping Patrick's hand. "So good to meet the one Remy's been waiting for, my dear."

"Thank you. I am blessed to have been found."

"Who wants a sherry?" Remy moved to the stand where his best decanter had been filled and turned out with small glasses.

Patrick served as he poured, then his *bébé* went to stand with Jean, discussing some of the volumes on his bookshelf.

"So, tell me why I'm here," Lionel demanded with no further pleasantries. "You're happy, but I sense worry as well."

"I require your assistance, *mes amis*. I have a concern."

"Of course," Isaiah said. "All you have to do is ask."

Remy smiled, his palms sweating. "Please, come sit."

They sat together in the high-backed chairs, the four of them forming a circle, quite unintentionally. Nonetheless, it was appropriate.

"I have been having moments, flashes of a talent I have never evinced before." No sense mincing words.

"Do tell." Lionel's eyes lit up, the interest immediate and prurient.

Isaiah poked Lionel in the ribs. "You be good."

"Where's the fun in that?"

Andrew rolled his eyes. "Doing what, Remy?"

"I can hear Patrick's thoughts. It was dull at first, but now, it is clear as a bell."

Lionel frowned. "Can you do it deliberately, or is it only in snatches?"

"I can speak to him. Watch." *Bébé, bring me the sherry?*

Patrick immediately turned to bring him the decanter. "Would you like me to pour, Remy?"

"Thank you, *bébé*. Please."

Patrick poured out, then studied their faces. *Holler if you need me, Sir. I'm just a thought away.* He rejoined Jean at the other end of the room.

"See? How is this possible? How can I hear him? How can he hear me? Neither of us are telepaths."

"No…" Andrew frowned. "But you are lovers, and I would say as unique a pair as Samuel and Joseph."

Lionel nodded. "Indeed. Have either of you heard anyone else?"

"*Non*. Not even a peep." And thank God for that.

"Then what exactly is the problem?"

Andrew snorted. "So pragmatic. I think I understand. You worry you'll begin to hear others."

"Indeed. That can drive a man mad. You know that I have only the barest talent, after all."

"Nonsense." The harsh words were his Patrick, voice snapping out and reminding him that, in another life, Patrick had been an officer. "You were made for me. You've said as such. Do not lessen that by saying it is a bare talent."

His cheeks heated, the rebuke hitting home. "I didn't mean to upset, *bébé*."

"It is not upset, sir. I need you, simple as that."

Isaiah chuckled. "That does seem cut and dried."

"Indeed." Lionel met his eyes. "Have you considered that your particular talent waited to fulfill itself until Patrick needed it? He is a beacon and you seem to be the only person to control it."

"I have thought of that, yes." He looked again to Patrick, who was his light in the dark as he was Patrick's focus.

"Thank all that's holy that he found you, then, or he'd have sunk himself and a bunch of people with him." Isaiah clapped him on the arm.

"Yes." His chest felt looser, his breath coming easier. All he had to do was focus on Patrick, just as he asked his boy to do on him.

Andrew held out a hand to him. "There's an easy way to solve this. Take my hand and try to read my thoughts."

Oh *dieu*. He didn't know if he wanted to do that. Still, as much as he didn't want to know, his fear of the unknown was worse, so he reached out.

Andrew took his hand in a warm, firm grip.

Can you hear me? Remy sent the thought with all the force he could.

Andrew never blinked, his patient, kind expression of waiting never changing.

So he tried to hear Andrew, but all he heard was Patrick's worry that he would give himself a headache. He chuckled, then shook his head.

Andrew nodded, releasing him. "No, Remy. You're no mind reader, else you would hear what I thought to you and be angry."

He let one eyebrow lift but, in truth, he was tickled. This was what he wished—to hear nothing but his beloved *bébé*.

Lionel nodded, sober now instead of sarcastic. "Andrew would tell you if he felt anything at all. Any use of a new talent."

"Well, good." Isaiah raised his one usable arm in a toast. "To actually having dinner."

"Indeed," Jean crowed. "I's starved."

Patrick hugged Jean lightly. "And talked out about books, I'll wager."

"You learned men, you's obsessed with the books."

Remy laughed aloud. "There are some with pictures you'll like, Jean. We'll look again after supper." He reached for Patrick's hand.

Solid and firm, his lover took it, their shoulders brushing together.

Germain appeared, announcing, "Dinner is served, Master Remy."

"Shall we?" He motioned to the door. "I believe we have a lovely meal ahead of us."

Andrew and Lionel linked arms. "Oysters?"

"However did you guess?" He laughed, and he swore he felt the barest caress to his balls.

Patrick was earning himself quite the punishment later on. Remy had a feeling neither one of them was going to be very patient.

Luckily, they had only to travel upstairs to their bedchambers once their company was gone, if they waited that long.

With this set of friends, there was no telling what dessert might bring.